# It Ruins Me

## Betrayal
### Book 3

## Penelope Sky

Hartwick Publishing

Hartwick Publishing

**It Ruins Me**

Copyright © 2024 by Penelope Sky

All rights reserved.

# Contents

# Chapter 1

## *Axel*

It was a cold night, the fog flooding the cities and the streets. It pressed up against my window and masked the views of the Duomo lit up in the distance. The fire was in the hearth, hot like a summer desert that was unwelcome when my temperature already ran so high. My elbow was propped on the armrest, and I stared at nothing in particular, ignoring both my cigar and the drink on the table.

Theo sat with me, his cheek against his closed knuckles, his eyes on the fire.

I wasn't in the mood for conversation, so silence was fine by me.

Several days had passed, and Scarlett's bruising had started to fade. It had been the worst the next day, all the signs of trauma amplified in the morning. It was hard to look at her, not because she wasn't beautiful, but because I knew how hard they'd hit her.

If she hadn't been smart enough to drop her location, she'd be dead right now.

I'd be a fucking widower.

Theo turned his head slightly and looked at me.

My eyes shifted to meet his.

"We can cancel."

I gave a slight shake of my head. "No. Life goes on."

"I can just meet with him."

"I'm not going to kill him."

"You sure?"

My stare hardened. "Why do you think you're here?"

"I'll keep you on your best behavior." The corner of his mouth rose in a smile. "How is she?"

"She's fine." She didn't complain about the pain. Did her best to cover it with makeup for my benefit—*so I wouldn't have to look at it.* But the air between us had been tense, not just because of the shit that had gone down, but because I'd told her I loved her and forced her to acknowledge it. "She's a tough woman."

"I'm sure it gave her a reality check."

"Yes...it did." A single moment had changed her attitude about this world, given her a bitter taste of reality. While I was relieved she took it seriously, it also hurt to see the defeated look in her eyes. Her ambition was snuffed out like a low-burning candle...and now all that remained was the smoke.

Aldo entered the parlor. "Dante is here to see you, sir."

I sucked in a slow breath. "Show him in."

Aldo left to fetch my favorite person.

Theo grabbed his glass, shook the ice, and took a drink.

Dante entered a moment later, his face still discolored from the hits he'd taken. I hit him the hardest, making him slam against the wall and crumple to the floor like a rag doll. We hadn't gotten along since the night he'd threatened me to stay away from his daughter, but that dislike had intensified into the strongest form of hate. He'd be dead right now if I didn't love his daughter.

He looked at Theo longer than necessary as he took a seat. He unbuttoned his jacket before his eyes shifted to me. It was a simple look across the table, but the moment our eyes locked, there was a fiery exchange of rage.

Silence stretched, and so did the stare.

Theo broke the tension. "There will be no bloodshed tonight." He grabbed a cigar and lit up. "Not when we have too much shit to do." He puffed on the end a couple seconds, getting the ashes to burn at the tip and start to produce the flavorful smoke. "I've halted upcoming orders because production has stopped, so we need to mitigate this before it turns into a serious problem. You know how upset people get when they're denied what they want." He shifted his look back and forth between us.

I was slumped in the armchair, wearing my sweatpants and a long-sleeved tee, my wife upstairs and unaware that her father had come for a visit. These meetings used to take place on his turf, but now that he was my bitch, they took place on mine.

Dante finally withdrew his gaze. "We'll need to find another supplier. The Colombians won't do business with us after we killed their men."

I wanted to wring his fucking neck for what he'd done, for nearly getting my baby killed. It was hard to sit in the same room with him, even if we were only discussing business. "You don't know that."

His eyes came back to me. "In fact, we should prepare for retaliation."

"The Colombians are going to come all the way over here to start shit?" Theo asked incredulously. "I find that unlikely."

"You never heard of hit men?" Dante asked. "We should have just given them what they wanted." His accusation turned back to me, potent and throbbing. "But you had to have a fucking ego—"

"I'd rather have an ego than be a fucking liar and a fucking psychopath."

Dante moved both of his arms to the armrests as he stared at me.

"She'll see your true colors." I relished the day he was no longer in our lives, either because he was dead or ostracized. "You'll learn."

"I sincerely hope not," he said calmly. "Because you know what those consequences will be."

I cocked my head. "Did you just threaten me?"

"I'm simply reminding you—"

"Not to tell her how worthless you are. But I can't control her figuring it out on her own, and with the way you've been conducting yourself, she's going to figure that out real quick."

Theo enjoyed his cigar as we went back and forth. "Gentlemen, let's focus on business." He held the cigar between his loose fingers as his arm rested over the back of the couch. "We need to arrange a meeting with the Colombians. I agree with Axel that we shouldn't make assumptions about the state of that relationship. Second to the US, we're their biggest client. We need them as much as they need us."

"Well," Dante said. "They were prepared to kill us for that ten percent—"

"They were prepared to hijack the business," Axel said. "And you were stupid enough to give them that chance. That's the second time you've dropped your guard and made yourself vulnerable to your enemies. And you say I'm the one with the ego..."

Dante brought his hands together and cracked his knuckles, like he wanted to punch me until I flew into the window behind me. "When was the first?"

"You really don't remember?" Theo turned to me. "Definitely didn't learn his lesson."

When Dante understood, his eyes dropped for a nanosecond.

"Had you by the fucking balls." I grabbed my own cigar and lit up because I needed something to soothe my anger.

Only booze and cigars could do that...and my wife. "Their mission failed. They don't have the business, and now they don't have the client. They're probably sitting on pallets of product they can't sell. Their production has probably already slowed because they've lost the demand. We need to set up a meeting."

"It's a family-run business," Dante said. "They aren't going to dismiss what happened—"

"Never assume anything," I snapped. "If they want to kill us, I'm sure they'll make that very clear."

Shaking his head in annoyance, Dante looked away. "I've been working with these guys for twenty years—and then you show up and that goes to shit."

"I've been in love with your daughter from the moment I saw her, and you've fucked that up every step of the way," I said. "So it looks like we're even."

As if my declaration of affection made him uncomfortable, he shifted his gaze to Theo.

Theo stared at the fire as he let the tension settle. "Then we'll set up a meeting and see where they stand. In the meantime, we need to find a backup supplier—"

"There is no one," Dante said coldly. "No one who can make a quality product and make it in such vast quantities. Trust me, I'm the expert on this—"

"We can do business with several suppliers," Theo said. "That can make up for the quantity."

"But the customers won't always get the same product," Dante argued. "They'll get one of three options—and customers want consistency."

"We'll make our own product if we must," I said. "That's probably something we should consider anyway."

"That's not possible," Dante said. "We can't fulfill that demand—"

"You're awfully pessimistic," Theo snapped. "I'm not sure how you built this business in the first place with an attitude like that."

Dante paused, his expression hardening into annoyance. "The Colombians have the luxury of space and privacy. We don't have that here. We can't open a factory in Tuscany. We're confined to what we have—which isn't much. I'm being the voice of reason here. The Colombians were the best partners we would ever hope to have—and you shit on all of that."

"You shit on your daughter when you brought her to that meeting—"

"Here we go again." Theo raised his voice. "Shut up—both of you."

I was tempted to pick up my chair and throw it at him.

Theo let a couple seconds of silence pass before he continued. "I think there's only one way to go about this. We meet the Colombians, tell them what happened, and offer the ten percent they originally asked for as a peace offering. If they're receptive, and I think they will be, then we move on."

Dante rolled his eyes. "If only we had just done that in the first place..."

"They obviously think you're a pussy bitch if they crossed you to begin with," Theo said. "And that's on you."

Dante snapped his neck as he turned to Theo.

"So, are we in agreement?" I asked. "If this doesn't work, we'll move to the next idea."

"Even if they agree," Dante said, "they'll probably plot to kill us anyway."

"I'm sure they will," Theo said. "And we'll be ready when they do."

"And when that time comes, we take them all out and put new people in charge," I said. "We'll clean house. If they weren't so far away, I would just take over their production altogether."

When I entered my bedroom, she was on the couch in her pajamas, ready for bed, with her makeup gone. The purple color of the bruising was distinct when it wasn't hidden under foundation and concealer. She did a remarkable job hiding it, but all that work went to waste when she washed it off before bed...and I had to look at it.

A blanket was pulled over her body, but she watched me with sharpness. Her eyes showed more than fatigue, a deeper level of defeat. It'd been that way the last couple of days, all of her personality and presence gone. "Where were you?"

"Downstairs with Theo." I omitted her father's presence on purpose.

She turned back to the TV.

"Why are you on the couch if you're tired?"

"Wanted to wait up for you."

She'd never done that before. "You don't need to do that, baby."

"I don't really have much of a choice." She looked at the TV before she rubbed the corner of her eye with her fingertip.

I turned off the TV before I approached her on the couch. "Come on."

She gave a quiet groan, slouched into the couch like her body had stopped working.

I felt like a father trying to get his kids to bed. I scooped her into my arms and lifted her against my chest, like she was an extra blanket I was stealing from the couch to put on the bed. I felt her arms hook around my neck and her cheek rest against my chest, so tired that she didn't voice a single protest.

I set her on the bed and tucked her in, seeing her sexy legs disappear underneath the crisp white sheet.

She gave a quiet sigh before her tired eyes looked at me.

I changed in the middle of the room, dropping my shirt and jeans on the floor and kicking off my boots underneath the armchair. The lamps were off, and the glasses of water were on the nightstands, placed by Aldo while Scarlett was crashed on the couch. I set my phone on the nightstand then got into bed beside her.

She'd been distant ever since that night, and while I wanted her every night, I let her be. But it was hard to sleep in that bed beside her, thinking about her sexy legs in those little shorts, and not do a damn thing about it. I was in love with this woman, from head to toe, and I wanted to make her mine at every opportunity.

She lay on the other side of the bed, her back to me, the sheets to her shoulder.

I stared at her silhouette in the dark, the outline of her petite waistline in the moonlight poking through the closed curtains. "Baby."

"Hmm?"

"I'm tired of this."

She remained quiet.

"I'm trying to be patient, but I've never been the patient type."

Nothing.

I shifted to her side of the bed, pressing my chest against her back and pulling her tight against me. My face was against her hair, smelling her shampoo and perfume mixed together in a floral scent. With that perky ass pressed against me, my dick hardened, wanting to dive between her folds and explore her wet paradise. My arm hooked over her chest to anchor her against me, to keep her secured tightly like she was light enough to float away. My lips brushed away the strap of her shirt so I could kiss her shoulder.

She remained still.

"Talk to me, baby."

There was a long stretch of silence, so long that it seemed like she would ignore me. "I'm still shaken up."

"There's nothing to be scared of."

"If you hadn't gotten there…" The sentence was never finished because she couldn't find the words…or didn't want to say them.

The implications were heavy in her voice. "But I did get there. Don't waste your heart worrying about what-ifs."

"It's more than that…"

"Then tell me."

She lay there for a moment before she rolled over, bringing her body toward mine so we were face-to-face.

I hooked her thigh over my hip and made her little shorts ride up until they fit like underwear. I squeezed one of her ass cheeks, feeling that perkiness right in the palm of my hand. I cared about her feelings, but it was hard to focus on her emotions when she was the sexiest little thing I'd ever laid eyes on. Ever since I'd manned up and told her I loved her, the steel bars that had restricted me had been shattered. I felt free, and all I wanted to do with that freedom was make love to her.

"I don't know who I am anymore." Her eyes carried a sadness so heavy even I couldn't lift it.

My desire suddenly evaporated. "Occupation and identity aren't the same thing. Your career is a part of who you are —but not *all* of who you are."

"But it's all I wanted for so long."

"You'll find something else to be passionate about. Like raising our children. When we have our babies, you aren't going to care about anything else anyway."

Her eyes dropped, moving to my chest. "I want to be more than just a mother."

"Then you'll find another passion."

"I'm just not sure how my father is going to take this."

That should be the least of her concerns, and the fact that she was pinned so hard under his thumb just pissed me off. "If he's anything but understanding, he's a fucking asshole. You value his opinion far more than you should. What do *you* want, baby?"

"I—I don't know."

"You can still have an empire, but it'll be a different kind of empire, one that's above the table rather than below it, that operates in the light of day instead of the shadows of midnight. I've always told you how much I love your cooking."

"You only like my cooking because it comes after sex."

I smirked. "I'm sure that helps, but I would eat your cooking at any time. I like your stuff better than my own chef's."

"I have the opposite opinion."

"I'd fire him and hire you in a heartbeat, but if you're too busy cooking, then you'll be too busy to fuck me, so that's not in my best interest."

A slight smile pulled at her lips, the light in her eyes masking the bruises that marked her beautiful skin.

I loved when she smiled. Did the strangest things to me. "What if we opened a restaurant?"

"I don't know..."

"You could build the menu from scratch. Teach the chefs how to make the dishes so they're the ones slaving away in the kitchen instead of you. Then you can work on the specials and do the books in the morning. It could be your business and have nothing to do with me at all."

"Well...I don't have the money for that sort of thing."

"Yes, you do." I tugged her closer to me, the two of us sharing a single pillow. "You know you do."

"I suggested this to my father, but he wasn't interested."

"Because he'd have no control over the situation, and all he cares about is—" I stopped at the annoyed look on her face. It was hard to mention her father without a tirade of ridicule, and it was something I seemed to get worse at—not better. "Just because he's not interested doesn't mean it's a bad idea."

"A restaurant is a big investment—"

"I told you we're billionaires."

"*You're* a billionaire. You earned that, not me."

"Baby, what's mine is yours."

"If I use your money to build my empire, then it's not my empire."

"Then pay me back." The idea of keeping receipts in a marriage seemed ridiculous, but I needed to give her a reason to get started, to feel better about herself rather than indebted to me.

"What if I can't?"

"Then you can pay me back in other ways..." I squeezed her ass.

"You know I do that for free every night."

"But it'll be fun for me to watch you work for it. Come on, let's do it."

"I don't know…"

"Baby, please."

"I know how upset my father will be."

"He's a grown-ass man," I said. "He'll get over it."

Her eyes dropped back to my chest. "I'll think about it."

# Chapter 2

## *Scarlett*

I waited until the bruises were healed to see my father. I didn't want him to suffer my appearance and the hefty price tag of guilt that came with it. Makeup had been a godsend during this week, but I couldn't wear it to bed without suffering a massive breakout, so Axel had to see me like that. At least it was dark.

It was afternoon, but it felt like morning with the heavy fog. It muffled the sounds of the city, brought an eerie silence to an epicenter of culture, food, and music. I was ready for spring, had been ready since the first day of winter. I walked past the guards on the property then entered the warmth of his villa, the fire burning in the parlor in anticipation of my arrival. I hung up my coat on the coatrack then moved farther into the room.

My father joined me moments later, dressed in a collared shirt and a jacket, looking professional even though he worked from home all day. "Hello, sweetheart." He didn't greet me with nearly the same affection and warmth. It'd been replaced by a heavy dose of hesitation and uncertainty. Even his hug was tentative, like the wrong touch could make me crumple into a pile on the rug.

My face was as it used to be, my makeup back to normal, my smile locked in place—but it wasn't enough. "How are you?" The last time I saw him had been that horrible night when we were both beaten bloody. Memories swept across my mind, and I imagined they swept across his too.

"Hungry?"

I felt a twinge of pain from his avoidance. "You know I'm always hungry."

"Good." He nodded toward the dining room. "Let's eat."

We took seats across from each other at the dining table, and Ramon immediately brought us lunch, soup and salad with a fresh basket of bread. Then he returned a moment later, placing a small pizza between us.

"Ooh...pizza." I grabbed a slice and put it on my plate before I even tried the salad.

"I knew you'd want something more substantial." He gave me a slight smile before he took another bite of his salad.

The conversation was like pushing a boulder uphill, but we eventually reached flat ground, and everything became easier. We talked about the weather, my father's new car, and the dinner he had with my uncle the other night. The tension ebbed as we finally stopped thinking about the night that had nearly gotten us killed.

"So...how are things at home?" He asked the question with averted eyes, his soup taking priority.

"It's a really big place for two people. We don't even visit the other parts of the house." We had to take two flights of stairs and walk down the hallway to reach the master suite, and it seemed so far away from everything else it was practically an island.

"He probably keeps it as an asset."

"Maybe," I said. "I hope you two have been getting along."

My father took a drink of his wine.

They barely tolerated each other in my presence. I couldn't imagine how they behaved in my absence. "There's something I wanted to talk to you about."

"I'm all ears." He set down his glass.

"After everything that happened..." I watched his eyes immediately flick away, like the mere suggestion was too much to swallow. "It makes me question this path, makes me wonder if this world is right for me."

He overcame his discomfort and looked at me. "What do you mean?"

I already felt his disappointment. "I'm not cut out for this sort of thing."

"How so?" He cocked his head slightly, his voice turning confident. "You killed one of them. Bashed another in the head with a chair."

"And was nearly choked to death..."

"I just think you're more capable than you realize."

"If Axel hadn't come, we'd both be dead." Well, my father would be dead. Worse things would be happening to me.

His stare continued until he took a slow breath. "What happened was extremely unfortunate. But I told Axel that we needed to honor the ten percent instead of playing games. All of that could have been avoided."

"Not everything can be avoided. Something else will happen someday...and I'm not prepared to deal with it."

My father stared at me for a long time, those intelligent eyes drilling past the surface to the oil in my soul. "It's okay to be scared—"

"I'm not sure why I ever thought I could fill your shoes. I'm not sure why you thought it either. I'm an easy target, and everyone who sees me is going to want to strike. I don't instill fear in my enemies the way Axel and Theo do."

"Don't let Axel manipulate you—"

"He doesn't manipulate me. This is how I feel, Dad."

He turned quiet, grabbing his glass and taking a drink. He swirled it before he returned it to the table. "So what are you saying exactly?"

I couldn't look at him as I said it. "I want out." I focused on the textured wood of the table, the lines sealed under the protective wax that made the surface soft to the touch. Silence was heavy, and the gray sunlight that burned through the windows suddenly felt too bright.

My father was still.

When he said nothing, my gaze lifted to him again.

All he did was stare, his eyes heavy in thought. "Sometimes I wonder if he did this on purpose."

"What?" I asked, unsure what that meant.

"He rejected their offer because he knew there would be a retaliation. A retaliation that would get me killed. But it worked out even better—because now you want nothing to do with the business."

"Dad, I think this would have happened anyway."

"I've been in this business a long time, and there's never been such a conflict."

"In the last couple of months, I've seen *a lot* of conflict." I swallowed, remembering the way I sat at that table in the restaurant and feared Theo and Axel were about to kill my father right before my very eyes. "I thought I was tough. I thought I could handle anything. But I realize now that I don't have the balls for this game."

His eyes stared into mine. "I inherently disagree."

"I've decided to open a restaurant instead."

Once my father realized this wasn't a discussion but an announcement, his body went rigid in the chair. His eyes dropped to the wine and lingered for a few seconds before he swallowed. He turned to the window, scratched the scruff at his neck, and then looked at me once again. "A restaurant." He barely spoke above a whisper, but those words conveyed so much resentment.

"Yes."

"A restaurant won't make you rich."

"Money isn't everything—"

"It is everything."

"Well, my husband is very rich, so..." I didn't view his money as my own, but as husband and wife, as partners, I would have to accept his wealth someday.

Both of his eyebrows lifted in surprise. "If this is what you've decided, then there's no reason to remain married to him."

My eyes were on my glass of wine, and they lifted when I heard what he said.

"You married him so we could reclaim our family business. If you've really decided to leave, then he's no longer useful to you. Your marital obligations have expired. Leave him. I'll give you the money to open the restaurant."

This conversation had taken an unexpected turn. "I asked you to open a restaurant before, but you rejected the idea—"

"Because the family business is a better idea."

"If I leave him..." I stared at the wineglass. "There's no incentive to keep you in the business." My eyes lifted to meet his again.

My father stared as he considered what I'd said. "You could ask. If you truly want nothing to do with this life, you'll need to get rid of Axel because he still ties you to his criminal activity. If someone wants to hurt him, they'll hurt you instead."

I hadn't thought of that.

"I don't think he'll cut me out of the business," he said. "Not when he needs me. Everything just went to shit with the Colombians, so we can't afford any more losses."

My stomach was tied in knots, and I felt a draft in the room even though none of the windows were cracked. I stared at the half-eaten pizza and avoided my father's stare.

"So, leave him, sweetheart."

---

When I came home, Axel was already on the couch, in nothing but his sweatpants and slightly damp hair. His schedule was random, so there were nights he'd be gone and days he wouldn't leave the couch.

"Hey, baby." One arm was over the back of the couch, and his powerful legs were stretched far apart. The table held his decanter of scotch and his empty glass. It wasn't even dinnertime yet, and he'd already started to drink.

"Hey..." I walked around the couch to put down my purse and slip off my heels.

"What was that?" he asked without turning around.

"What?"

"I expect a kiss when my loving wife comes home."

I left my heels on the floor before I moved into the living room and came around the edge of the couch. With my hand planted on the back of the couch, I leaned in and gave him a quick peck on the lips.

His big arm wrapped around me, and he dragged me into him, forcing me onto my back on the couch as he moved on top of me.

I tried to fight it, but when that heavy mass was on top of me, I knew I had no chance of escape. "What are you doing?"

He held himself on top of me. "Waiting for my wife to kiss me."

"I did kiss you—"

"Come on, baby. You can do better than that." He held himself above me, his eyes looking down at my lips in expectation of a passionate kiss. It'd been a week since we'd last had sex, and I knew he was anxious to resume those evenings where we fucked all night.

"I just had a long day."

"Yeah?" he asked, his eyes still on my lips. "Let me help you forget about it." He dipped his head and kissed me, a slow kiss that wasn't demanding or aggressive, just easy and gentle. He touched my lips with his as his hand slid into my hair, his fingers stroking the soft strands. When he felt the enthusiasm from my lips, he deepened the kiss, making it harder, making it faster.

My stressful day was erased by a slow ache in my stomach, an ache that turned into a burn that stretched to other parts of my body...especially between my thighs. My hands latched on to his thick arms before planting on his hard chest, feeling a concrete surface that was warm to the touch rather than cold. His tongue delved into my mouth and elicited a quiet moan from me, a moan I couldn't even remember making.

He tugged his sweatpants down over his ass so his cock could come free, tinted red and throbbing with desperation. Without breaking our kiss, he lifted my dress to my waist and exposed my thong before he pulled it free. It was tossed on the floor and underneath the coffee table.

He tugged me close and folded me, bringing our disproportionate bodies together so his hard dick could slide into my tightness. He dampened the head of his dick first then pushed inside, giving a hard thrust to burst past my opening and enter the wetness waiting for him. As he started to sink, he released the sexiest moan, like this was the best pussy he'd ever had.

Like I was the best he'd ever had.

He moved until there was nowhere else to go, until he hit my cervix and made me wince at the intrusion. His lips found mine again, and he kissed me as he started to move, taking it nice and slow, prioritizing our kiss over the reunion of our bodies.

My arms hooked around his back, and my nails dug deep to anchor myself in place as he thrust into me, as his big dick made itself right at home after our short dry spell. I moaned against his lips, interrupting our kiss when the pleasure became too much. I panted against his mouth, my hips rocking, my desperation bursting from nowhere.

"Fuck, Pretty." His fingers fisted my hair tighter, and he pulled his lips away because now he wanted to fuck me harder. "I missed this pussy."

---

We sat across from each other at the dining table.

Aldo had delivered dinner from downstairs, a three-course meal on shiny platters. There was also an expensive bottle of wine for us to share. I noticed desserts were never a part of the menu, like they were off-limits.

Axel had put his sweatpants back on but was still shirtless, hard as a rock even when in a seated position. He never touched the basket of bread sitting there, and his dinner was usually meat and vegetables…pretty boring. But that boring lifestyle made him cut like the finest piece of beef, so I didn't mind.

"You seemed down when you walked in." His plate was empty because he'd already finished his dinner. Whenever food was placed in front of him, his elbows were on the table and he inhaled the meal like a caveman.

"Oh…I was with my father."

"Figures." He drank from his wineglass as he stared at me across the table.

"We had lunch."

"What was on the menu? Bullshit?"

I spun my fork in my pasta, eyes down. "If you're going to act like that, then I'll just keep it to myself."

He gave a sigh before he drank from his glass again. "Continue."

I took a bite of the pasta and savored it before I answered. "I told him how I felt."

"And?"

"He understood…as best as he could."

"Don't let his disappointment affect you."

"He told me there's been a lot of conflict lately, but in his long career, it's usually easy and peaceful."

"It's a dangerous business," he said. "To downplay that is to lie."

"He's just sharing his experience—"

"Why do you defend him?" He slouched in the chair, elbows on the armrests. "You confided your fears to your father, and he basically told you to dust yourself off and get back out there."

"I'm not defending him," I said. "And can we ever discuss my father without it turning into this?"

His fingers came together in front of him, his stare annoyed. "Probably not."

"I told him I was thinking of opening a restaurant."

"And?"

I shrugged. "He didn't have much to say."

"At least he accepted your decision. That's more than I expected."

The conversation went deeper than that, and I wasn't sure why I was tempted to share it. "He said if I don't want the business...then there's no reason for me to stay married to you." Once the words were out into the ether, tension filled the room and masked the aroma of the meal we'd just finished.

Axel didn't change his posture or his stare, rigid and hard as stone.

I wasn't sure what he would say to that, but I didn't think he would say nothing.

I continued to withstand his stare, absorbing the tension until it made me feel toxic.

"Is that what you want?" His deep voice broke the silence, calm despite the malice in his expression.

"My father thinks you would keep him as a partner if I did decide to leave." I didn't phrase it as a question, afraid of being too forward about the situation.

He cocked his head slightly, continuing to look at me with coldness. "Let's just say I did keep him on... What would you do?"

Now the air was too thick to breathe. It was like hot steam filling my lungs, so heavy that I couldn't get the oxygen that I needed. "I don't like to speak in hypotheticals—"

"I'll keep him on if you leave. There." He massaged his knuckles, his focused stare trained on me like a scope from a sniper. "No more hypotheticals."

The stakes had just been raised, and I felt like I'd walked into a trap.

"What's it going to be, baby?"

Now that I wanted nothing to do with the business, I had no reason to be there anymore. I could walk away whenever I wanted...start over with someone new...move back in to my old apartment. I'd tried so hard to avoid Axel when we were first married, but now my old life sounded pathetic...and miserable. "I want to stay."

He continued to massage his knuckles as he looked away, his face turning toward the window that showed the dim lights through the heavy fog. Then a slight smile moved over his lips. "You knew how I felt before I said a word." He turned back to me, arrogance in his stare. "Because you felt it. Felt it in my gaze. Felt it in my obsession. My commitment, passion, and words. That's how you know it's real, when it exists without ever being spoken. Now I know you feel the same way."

I felt like a deer in the headlights. Felt like my diary had been opened and read from cover to cover. All my secrets were exposed for everyone to see—and Axel had a fucking microscope.

"So why don't you be a man and say it?" He stopped massaging his knuckles, his joined hands resting against his bottom lip.

My eyes dropped to the table between us, the goose bumps like hills and mountains up my arms. My heart beat at a quicker pace, like I was running rather than sitting in place. His stare was too much, like the sun was right in my face as I tried to drive.

"Come on, baby..."

My eyes lifted to meet his, and the same old flashbacks swept across my mind, picturing him with Cassandra, a woman who looked so different from me that I didn't understand how he could be attracted to us both. It filled me with as much pain now as it had the moment it happened. It toughened my heart and covered it with scales. "My father said as long as you're associated with the business, I would be associated with it. And the best way to hurt you...is to hurt me."

The arrogance was slowly wiped away.

"So, I'll never be safe."

"You're always safe with me." His voice dropped, turning quieter and stronger at the same time. "I would never let anything happen to you. Ever."

"If I hadn't sent you my location—"

"You called for help. I came."

My eyes were down again. "It'll still be a part of my life, even if I have nothing to do with it."

He lowered his hands and moved closer to the table, his elbows resting on the surface, his dirty plate still there. "If you don't want a divorce, then what do you want?"

My eyes reached his. "Would you be willing to...walk away?"

His eyes shifted back and forth between mine. "Is this hypothetical, or are you actually asking me?"

"Does it matter?"

"It does," he said. "Here are the two answers. Hypothetically, I would do anything to make you happy. I already planned on leaving this line of business when I had a family, so I've always been willing to make the sacrifice. I would make it for them—and I would make it for you."

I'd expected resistance. Outright refusal. Some long-winded speech.

"Now, if you're actually asking me, right here and right now, I would say I need more time. I just started this partnership with Theo, and everything has gone to shit. I can't jump ship right now, not after what he did for me. I would need six months to a year before I could realistically sever ties. But the answer is yes."

It was a reasonable response, so reasonable that I couldn't ask for more. "There's something else..."

"Tell me."

I had a feeling he wouldn't be as agreeable to this request. "That business means a lot to my father, and I know how devastated he is that you've taken it from him. You know I want to stay, so would you be willing to give it back to him?"

His expression hardly changed, but it somehow felt like an earthquake.

"If you'd be willing to leave it for me, why not just give it back to him?"

He looked away, giving a slight shake of his head.

"Axel—"

"No."

"It means nothing to you—"

"It means everything to me because it means everything to him," he snapped. "He knew how I felt about you, and he didn't hesitate to use that against me. I will never give it back to him. Not for anything—even you."

I swallowed, slapped by the disappointment. "What do you mean, he knew how you felt about me and used it against you?"

He gave a heavy sigh. "It doesn't matter now." He turned to look at me again. "I will give up the world for you—but I will give up nothing for him."

"If we want to stay together, I'd like it if the two of you got along. I think giving him back the business would be a great gesture for the two of you to start a new relationship. You and I can run our restaurant together and start a family—"

"No."

"Axel." I tried to keep my voice as light as possible. "He's never going to go away. He'll always be a part of my life. There's nothing you can do about that. So you may as well try...to make things better."

He looked out the window again. "If only you knew..."

"Knew what?"

All he did was shake his head.

"Just think about it...is all I ask."

# Chapter 3

## *Axel*

I secured the vest across my body. It only weighed ten pounds, but it was thick enough to stop a bullet or a knife. When I'd gone to the factory to save my wife, I hadn't had the time to put it on, so I'd gone in blind and vulnerable. Now I had something to live for, so I was careful to watch my back and my front.

I hadn't seen Scarlett most of the day, so I texted her. *Baby, where are you?*

*In the kitchen.*

I went downstairs to the bottom floor and into the second kitchen in the rear. It'd been a long time since I'd had a party, but whenever I did, people liked to congregate in the kitchen and on the barstools. So, I had a kitchen for entertaining and a kitchen for the actual cooking. I stepped inside and found the kitchen island covered with ingredients and hot pans on the stove. It smelled divine, and my stomach tightened even though I'd already had dinner.

I leaned against the counter and stared at her.

She stirred the contents of one pan before she moved to the other and flipped a piece of chicken.

"I wish I'd known you were cooking. Would have skipped dinner."

She gave a slight flinch like she didn't know I was there. "Shit, you scared me."

"I just asked where you were. You didn't think I was on my way?"

"Guess I was distracted." She finished what she was doing before she dragged her dirty hands down the front of her apron.

"What are you making?"

"I got this idea for a recipe and wanted to try it out." She moved to the sink and washed her hands free of the oil and butter that had caked her fingers. "The more I think about it, the more excited I get about running a restaurant. How cool would it be if I got a Michelin star?"

"That would be cool," I said. "But you already have the Michelin star in fucking, and no one likes an overachiever."

She rolled her eyes, but my comment made her smile.

I smiled too.

She dried her hands before she leaned against the counter and looked at me.

There were moments like this when the light hit her in just the perfect way that her eyes shone like emeralds. Her skin had a natural glow that made her look like living gold. The world got quiet, and I knew I could stare at her forever. "I'm going out tonight. Not sure when I'll be back."

"Oh..."

Ever since I'd gotten married, I'd rearranged my schedule to be home with her in the evenings. I didn't like the idea of her sleeping alone in my bed. Abandoning her during the most vulnerable time of the day made me feel like an inadequate husband. But tonight couldn't be helped.

"Some of my guys are going to be on the property while I'm gone. I ask that you don't leave."

"Okay...now you're making me worry."

"Nothing to worry about."

"You've never left me with a small army before."

"After what happened with your father, I'd rather be cautious."

Her arms crossed over her chest. "That means you're doing something dangerous tonight."

"Everything I do is dangerous."

"No, it's not," she snapped. "Most of the time, you attend snobby cocktail parties and make deals in the back room."

"Baby, it'll be fine."

She ignored what I said. "What are you doing?"

"I have a meeting with the Colombians."

"The ones who just tried to kill me?" she asked incredulously.

"Yes."

"Jesus… Life goes on, doesn't it?" Her arms tightened over her chest, and she gave a sigh.

"They're the only supplier that can meet our standards of quality and our quota. It's worth trying to mend the relationship."

"What if you're walking into a trap?"

"Then they're walking into a trap too."

Her eyes were furious now, bright and agitated, but they somehow gave her this irresistible beauty. "I don't like this."

"It'll be alright."

"These men should be with you, not me."

"I've got my guys, baby."

She continued to look flustered, her food cooking on the stove without her attention. The smell started to change, like it was burning, but she didn't seem to notice or care. "Can't this happen on the phone?"

I gave a slight smile. "No."

"Axel, I don't like this—"

"It'll be fine."

"My father is going with you?"

I nodded. That rat was always a step behind me.

"And Theo?"

I still didn't like it when she mentioned my brother, because I knew she was attracted to him, had invited him into the bed where I used to sleep. It was immature and childish, but it still bothered me to this day. "Yes."

"This could be a plot to get their revenge—"

"They're our biggest supplier, but we're their biggest client. We need each other."

"How do you know they'll be so reasonable?"

"I don't. But it's stupid to attack someone when they're prepared for it."

She looked at the stove, seeing her culinary delicacy beginning to burn from being exposed to the heat too long. She turned off the burners and took the pans off the heat so the oil would rest.

"I'm sorry if I ruined your project."

"I don't give a shit about the food." She wiped her hands on the apron before she turned back to me. "Just don't want to burn down the house."

I leaned against the counter as I looked at her, seeing all the distress on her beautiful face, the way she struggled to accept what I was about to do.

"Text me the second you're on your way home."

"I will."

"Please be careful."

"Always."

Her eyes were full of despair, despair that couldn't be resolved until I walked back through the door. They continued to plead with me, like her silent begging would make me decide to bow out and let the guys go without me.

But I was no coward. "I'll be back in a couple of hours."

"*Hours?*" she asked, dismayed.

"Sorry, baby." I moved to her, my hands gripping her arms before cupping her face. "I'll be hungry by the time I get back. Make me something."

Her eyes were focused on my chest, heavy in sadness.

I brought her close and kissed her forehead before I pulled her into me, my chin resting on the top of her head. After my divorce, I hadn't thought I'd ever want to be married again, to be vulnerable to another woman's talons of betrayal. But I loved it. Loved every moment of it—even the hard parts.

---

We met in the heart of Tuscany, in a villa on twenty acres of property, far away from everyone and everything. It was one of my properties, a place I used when Florence became too busy in the summertime. But I hadn't been there in a long time.

"Where's Russell?" Theo asked when we pulled up to the villa. The lights in the three-story villa were on. The landscape lights were on too, showing the majesty of the property. Most of the greenery was dead from winter's bite, and the jasmine flowers wouldn't bloom again until spring. But it was breathtaking, nonetheless.

"I left him with Scarlett."

"He's your best guy."

I got out of the car and walked up to the property. "That's why I left him."

Dante hadn't said a word since he'd gotten in the car. Hardly looked at me, the accusation heavy in his energy.

We moved to the back patio, the stream of lights across the terrace bathing the potted trees in a glow. The fountain was on, the sound of running water soothing. The pool was in the distance, ice-cold in the season.

I'd have to bring Scarlett here in the summertime.

A table with several chairs was set up on the patio, so we took a seat.

The guards were placed around the property, carrying machine guns. The ones inside were snipers, so they could take out the guys through the windows. It was a chilly night, the fog visible even in the darkness, but to me, it was refreshing.

One of the guys lit the bonfires, so soon, the terrace was bright and filled with a bit of warmth.

Theo looked at his phone for a few minutes before he slipped it into the pocket of his coat.

Dante still hadn't said a word, his eyes on the closest bonfire.

I preferred Dante quiet, so I didn't coax him into conversation.

Minutes passed and nothing happened.

Theo lifted his sleeve and looked at his watch. "They're late."

Dante kept his eyes on the fire. "They are coming all the way from Colombia."

"Doesn't matter," I said. "You want to do business with us, then be on time."

"Maybe they don't want to do business," Dante said coldly. "Just going to show up and blow us all to hell."

Theo turned to me. "Is he always this pessimistic?"

"Yep," I said. "Debbie Downer."

Dante gave us both a razor-sharp stare.

Theo decided to make small talk. "How are things with the wife?"

"Good," I said. "Whenever her father isn't meddling, it's always good."

Dante said nothing to that.

A moment later, one of the guards raised his hand and gestured to me across the terrace.

"It's showtime," I said.

"I've got backup if we need it," Theo said. "Just down the road."

Dante stayed silent.

Footsteps were audible, even over the noise of the fountain, before they became visible. A group of men approached, five of them in total, all dressed in t-shirts like they didn't take our winter weather seriously. Two of them had face tattoos, and another one had eyes so wide it looked like he had a direct view into the horrors of the underworld.

We didn't rise from our chairs. Just watched them with indifferent eyes.

They moved to the other side of the bonfire, where the chairs were scattered. They dropped into them and stared at us, taking several moments to evaluate us as opponents rather than business partners.

My guys had checked them not only for weapons, but for explosives wired to their clothing, in case this was a suicide bombing. We'd even installed a metal detector to catch anything they could have. Even if it was an innocent piercing, it had to go.

The standoff ensued, them sizing us up as we did the same in return.

I was the one to break the silence. "Tensions are heavy. Hatred is rooted in your bones. It's understandable. But none of that would have happened if Christian hadn't foolishly attempted to take a business from men he greatly underestimated—and touch one of their wives. I'm not sorry he's dead, not after he made my wife bleed, but I am sorry that our thriving partnership has turned to shit."

The one in the middle stared at me harder than the others, like he had an imaginary knife to my throat. He had tattoos in the corners of his eyes.

"We have two options here. We can let bygones be bygones and continue our partnership that has flourished for twenty years—or we can start a war. What do you want to do? Avenge a family member who crossed us or make money hand over fist?" I scanned them all, looking for reactions and weaknesses.

None of them looked at one another. None of them whispered to one another. They seemed to have had a game plan before they'd walked in. The one in the middle had his mouth covered with his hand, but he dropped it to speak. "An apology would be nice."

"An apology for what?" I asked coldly.

Dante turned to me but didn't say anything.

The man scooted forward to the edge of his chair. "We asked for ten percent—and you disrespected us."

"Ten percent is awfully generous when you aren't a part of this business."

"Our product has allowed you to have a business," he snapped. "It's a small price to pay to stand on our spines. My cousin would still be alive if you'd just honored the request."

"No," I barked. "He would still be alive if he hadn't threatened to rape my wife and nearly broke her nose. That's why he's fucking dead. And I'd kill him again—right in front of you—for what he did."

"Axel." Dante spoke under his breath.

The Colombian's stare remained composed, but there was a flare to his nostrils he couldn't restrain.

"However," Theo said, jumping in to mitigate the damage I'd caused. "We would like to offer the ten percent and include you as a partner in the business going forward, as a sign of respect and sympathy. Business would continue as it always has, but you'll receive a bigger piece of the pie. Do you accept?"

My temper had gotten the best of me, but I couldn't see straight when it came to Scarlett. I would always remember her bloody face because it was carved into the backs of my eyes. The image appeared in my dreams, in the quiet moments as I sat in front of the fire, in the times that I felt at peace. It was a sick torment.

Their spokesperson looked down at the fire, slouching back into his chair, arms hanging down in a relaxed pose.

If he tried to negotiate for more, he would be denied, so I hoped he wouldn't waste his time with that.

"If you'd just offered this in the first place, my cousin would be alive right now." His eyes lifted to look at me, daggers in that stare. "All you had to do was agree, but you chose to be arrogant."

"Christian had a lot of other threads he could have pulled to get what he wanted," Dante said. "He could have left the meeting and withdrawn his product until we were forced to come to the negotiation table. Trying to take the business, along with my daughter and me, was not the right hand to play. Don't blame us for your cousin's foolishness. What happened was tragic, but we are in no way responsible for the bloodshed. The smart thing to do is move forward and continue this business arrangement. It's obvious we need one another. We need you as our supplier, and you need us as your biggest client. Let's learn from the past and not squander millions because of our tempers."

Moments like this reminded me that Dante wasn't completely useless. Unlike me, he could keep his temper, or at least halt it until the appropriate moment. When his eye was on the prize, he was focused like the point of a laser.

The Colombian considered the offer in silence before he straightened in his chair. "I accept your offer."

"Great," Dante said. "We are glad to continue this partnership—"

"But I want him dead." The guy continued to stare at me, aiming a bullet at my face without a gun. "An eye for an eye."

I knew there would be some stupid stipulation. The Colombians were all about family, and to think they would let Christian's death go unpaid was unrealistic. But asking for my head was more than unrealistic—it was ridiculous.

"I shoot him—and we have a deal." He looked to Theo and Dante for agreement.

I knew Theo wouldn't fold on me. This would work out perfectly for Dante, however.

"Then we have no deal," Theo said. "The only reason Axel was there was because his wife called for help. You can blame Axel for pulling the trigger, but his actions were reactionary. Christian was the one who instigated the whole thing."

"You're prepared to lose this partnership?" His eyes flicked back to me. "For him?"

"Yes," Theo said immediately. "It'll take time, but you can be replaced. My brother can't be."

He looked at Dante next. "You agree with this?"

Dante remained quiet for several seconds, his eyes on the bonfire, his legs crossed. "It doesn't matter whether I do or not. I'm outvoted."

"I still want to know your answer," he pressed, like he picked up on the tension between the two of us.

Dante gave a sigh. "I know my daughter cares for him... so no."

I wondered if that was really his answer or if he was being diplomatic because his vote didn't matter anyway.

The man gave a nod then clapped his hands against his thighs. "Then our business has concluded. Hopefully you can find a supplier to fulfill the demand."

"And hopefully you can find a client who can move product the way we can," I said. "It'd be a shame for all of that to go to waste."

The men rose from the chairs then left the terrace, moving between the buildings to the entrance of the villa so they could pile into their cars and drive off.

We sat there, rigid in our seats, our muscles stiff from the cold. Minutes of silence passed.

I texted Scarlett because I'd promised I would. *Meeting is over. I'll head home soon.*

Her message was instantaneous, like she'd been staring at her phone, waiting for my dots to appear. *Thank you.*

Dante was the first to speak. "Well, that was a shitshow."

"They're bluffing," Theo said. "We can always find a way to make more product, but they can't sell in this territory without being butchered. They're walking away from a lot of money solely out of pride—and that's fucking stupid."

"Doesn't matter if it's stupid," Dante said. "If this isn't a bluff, it'll set us back a year."

"They'll cave," Theo said simply.

"And if they don't?" Dante asked.

"We'll shoot Axel in the head," Theo said sarcastically. "Problem solved."

Dante gave a sigh.

"I agree with Theo," I said. "It's a bluff."

"A stupid bluff," Theo said. "Like we're going to really shoot you."

"It's not about Axel or revenge," Dante said. "It's a power play."

"Which is a game," Theo said. "And I don't play games."

"Then we wait for them to contact us," I said. "In the meantime, we find an alternative. Who knows? Maybe we'll find something better than the partnership with the Colombians."

Theo rubbed his jawline. "That gives me an idea."

"Let's hear it." I could go for a cigar right now. It would be perfect in this evening chill.

"We pursue an alternative, whether it works or not, and when the Colombians come back to us, we say we've already found a new supplier. The only reason we would take them back is if they offered a better price. And then we bring them back to their original fee."

I released a short laugh. "Fuck, that would be hilarious."

"And stupid," Dante said. "You just said you don't play games."

"They made their power move," Theo said. "And I'll make mine."

"If that happens, we should just take the deal," Dante said. "Get back to our old lives."

"These guys would have killed you if Axel hadn't shown up." Theo sat up and pivoted in his chair, staring down Dante on the other side of me. "Did you ever think of that? That they would have tortured you until they got everything they wanted and then killed you? They would have raped and knocked up your daughter with a Colombian baby—"

"Don't." Dante looked at the bonfire, his face so hard all the veins in his temple and neck popped out. "Fucking don't..." His fingers tightened into a closed fist before he rested it against his lips.

I turned to Theo and shook my head slightly, telling him to back off because I could feel Dante's agony through the air, feel his combustive rage and his profound terror.

Theo listened and gave a nod. "They crossed you. And you should make them pay, Dante."

When I walked in the door, it was nearly two in the morning—but she was wide awake.

On the couch in her little silk shorts and one of my t-shirts, she looked exhausted from staying awake long past her bedtime, but she also looked happier than I'd ever seen her. Relief swept across her eyes, and she took a deep breath as she finally allowed her body to relax. "I'm so happy you're home." She left the couch and came to me, diving into my chest like it was a mattress and a pillow.

My arms circled her, and I held her close to me, my hand sliding up the baggy shirt to feel her skin against my fingertips. I held her there for a long time, letting her rest her cheek against my chest for as long as she needed.

She pulled away. "My father's okay?"

I nodded.

She breathed another sigh of relief. "How did it go?"

She'd decided to leave the business, so I wouldn't concern her with the details that didn't matter. "Fine. Did you make me something?"

"Do you ever think about anything besides my cooking?"

"Oh, baby," I said with a grin. "You know what else of yours I think about..."

She dropped her look, her cheeks immediately flushing like tomatoes ripe on the vine. "I made you chicken fricassee. It's a French stew."

"Sounds fancy."

"It's in the fridge downstairs," she said. "Take a shower, and I'll have it ready for you."

"Wow, it's nice having a wife."

She smirked as she headed for the door. "Be back soon."

I took a quick shower and scrubbed my hair dry with a towel before I pulled on a clean pair of shorts and walked into the dining room.

She had the bowl of stew on the table, the steam rising to the ceiling. She sat quietly, still looking tired but relaxed.

I sat across from her. "Go to bed, baby. You don't need to stay up with me."

"I want to see if you like it."

I scooped my spoon in the creamy stew and took a bite, immediately tasting the culmination of several flavors that blended together without overpowering the dish. The chicken was tender. As with all the things she cooked, it was a delicacy. "It's delicious like everything else you make."

"Really? I was thinking of having this on the winter menu."

"And I would order it."

She smiled. "You aren't just saying that?"

"No. If it sucked, I would tell you."

"Really?" she asked, her eyebrow cocked.

"Yes."

"You would look me in the face and tell me it sucked?"

"I would say it nicer than that, but yes."

"I find that hard to believe."

"I want your restaurant to be a success. I wouldn't let you make a fool out of yourself. But that doesn't matter because this shit is good and you have a gift in the kitchen." I took another bite then wiped my mouth with the napkin. "And the bedroom."

"That's awfully generous since I don't do much in the bedroom."

"Being sexy is your contribution." I continued to eat, arms on the table, feeling the cold fade away as the warmth filled my stomach.

She watched me eat in silence. "So, did the Colombians agree to come back?"

"Doesn't matter."

"What do you mean, it doesn't matter?"

"You said you wanted out."

"Doesn't mean I'm not curious."

When I took another bite, I took my time getting it down, trying to decide how to play this. "They said they weren't interested in continuing a partnership. But Theo thinks they'll change their minds."

"Why would they change their minds?"

"Because they'll realize they can't substitute us with another client or several clients. We move far more product than anyone else, and they fucking know it. And they can't take this territory themselves or partner with someone who can take this territory. After they bleed so much money, they'll come running back."

She gave a slight nod in agreement. "They need you more than you need them."

"Should have just left it alone."

"Men get greedy."

"They get stupid is more like it." I ate from the bowl until there was nothing left. It was warm and delicious, far better than anything my chef could make and better than anything I could order at a local restaurant. It shocked me that she had no professional training, that her approach to cooking was so natural and organic. No pun intended. "We should start looking around for a spot for the restaurant. Location is everything."

"I was thinking close to the market. People get hungry after they do their shopping."

"Then we'll start there," I said. "But first, let's go to bed. I need to thank you for the dinner you made me."

The flush moved into her cheeks again, but a smile was there too. "It's late. Let's go to sleep—"

"No, I want some dessert." I rose from the chair and came around the table to grab her. "Something sweet." I scooped her into my arms and lifted her from the chair to carry her to the bedroom. "Something pretty..."

---

It was almost dark when I arrived at Dante's property.

It was one of the darkest days of the year, so the light was gone just shy of five o' clock, and it was fitting for the occasion because anytime I was in this man's presence it felt like a nightmare. I was escorted into the parlor but not offered a refreshment, treated like an enemy rather than an ally who had saved his life.

He entered a moment later and took the seat across from me, the displeasure pulsing in his eyes like a flickering lightbulb. His arms were on the armrests, and he crossed his legs like he was a stuffy museum curator. "Have the Colombians reached out?"

"I'm not here to talk about business."

"Then what are you here to talk about?"

"You know what." There was one thing that connected us now. Or, I should say, *one person* who connected us. "I love Scarlett, and she knows I do because I told her." I'd told her when I should have told her sooner. Instead of playing it cool because it was too soon in the relationship to drop the L-bomb, I should have just straightened my spine and spoken my mind. "But she won't say it back...and I know why."

Dante had the presence of a statue—devoid of all emotion.

"I'm going to tell her everything."

His stonelike gaze hardened at the threat. His expressions were always subtle and nuanced because he kept his emotions the way he kept his cards—close to his chest. But the anger was unmistakable.

"As a courtesy, I'll give you the opportunity to speak to her first. Word it in whatever way you want to make yourself look as good as possible. I don't care. My agenda is not to show her what a horrible man you are, but to prove that I've always been faithful to her, that she's all I've ever wanted since the moment I met her. I'm tired of living with this cloud over my head and watching it pour down on our sunshine."

Dante said nothing, bringing his hands close together, wearing a ring on each hand. "I meant what I said. Tell her —and your parents are dead."

I was surprised, but not entirely so. "I saved your ass, Dante."

"My ass wouldn't have needed to be saved if you'd just given them the ten percent. I'm not an idiot. I know that was on purpose."

"If I wanted to kill you, I would just do it myself," I said. "In fact, I'd prefer it."

His expression remained hard.

"I saved your daughter. You at least owe me that."

"Again, you decide to fuck with the Colombians—"

"And you decided to bring her there. That's all on you, Dante. As manipulative and deceitful as I think you are, I know you love your daughter very much." I saw it in the way emotion overcame him in certain moments, the way he'd begged for her life instead of trying to save his own.

He did some shitty things, but if it came down to her or him, he would take the bullet so she could walk away. "Tell her, or I will."

"Then I'll shoot both of your parents through the fucking eye."

If only Scarlett knew half the shit that came out of his mouth. "I can tell Scarlett the truth, and if something happens to my parents, you're the cause of it. You lose your daughter."

"Then I may as well take your parents so we're even."

I hadn't expected that at all. "You would let innocent people die just to be spiteful?"

"I don't give a shit about innocent people," he snapped. "Tell Scarlett the truth, but know that it'll come at a price. If I lose my family, you lose yours. So you have to decide what's more important to you. Your marriage or your parents."

This man really was a sick fuck. "I've proven myself loyal to your daughter. It would suit my best interests if I killed you, and while I could snuff out your life without her ever suspecting me, I would never hurt her like that. I would never deprive her of her father. I wish you would grant me the same respect by supporting my marriage to your daughter. She deserves to know the truth—that I would never even look at another woman."

He blinked a few times, his stare resembling boredom. "As there's no way to accomplish that without incriminating myself, I can't help you. You seemed to have done a remarkable job earning her trust, because she's told me how much she cares for you." He said it with a hint of disdain, like it made him sick to know that her feelings for me were genuine.

"She married me because she felt like she had to," I said. "But now she's married to me because she wants to be. I know that must kill you."

He returned to his stoniness, looking at me like he felt nothing at all.

"You know I'm innocent. You know I didn't do any of the things I was accused of."

"Found guilty of. Big difference, Axel."

"You think your daughter would love me if any of that shit were true? If I ever treated her that way?"

"She's never said she loves you. You're assuming."

"I know she does," I said softly. "I told her she could leave me if she wanted, that I would continue this business with you, just to see what she would say. And you know what?

She decided to stay. If that's not love, I don't know what is."

Now he looked away, knowing he was defeated.

"I'm going to spend the rest of my life with her, Dante."

He continued to avoid my eyes.

"We're going to open a restaurant together. Have a family together. Do it all together. I know I have no other choice but to accept you as an accessory to our lives. Why can't you do the same for me?"

His stare came back. "It's clear that I tolerate you."

"I deserve to be more than tolerated. I deserve to be fucking celebrated for the way I treat your daughter. I do all the gentlemanly bullshit like open doors and pull out chairs, but I do a lot more than that, like remain faithful to her because I want to be faithful to her, protect her with my life the way I did when I faced the Colombians without a bulletproof vest. I fucking love your daughter, and you should be grateful that I care for her so deeply. It's a dream come true, if you ask me."

"You make it sound like she can't do better."

"No man will ever love her as much as I do," I said. "I loved her the moment I saw her."

Dante looked away again. "What do you want from me?"

"Tell her the truth."

"I can't."

"I'll tell her to forgive you, and she will. It might take some time, but it'll happen."

"Not worth the risk."

"Dante—"

"Axel." He looked at me again. "The answer is no. I won't change my mind. Do what you want, just remember what the consequences will be. There's nothing left to discuss here, so you can show yourself out."

# Chapter 4

## *Scarlett*

I walked into the vacant space, the floor empty of tables and chairs, the back counter where the bar was located covered in old dust. Passersby moved down the street, carrying their groceries, sandwiches, or gelato. Pino's, the sandwich shop my father and I had visited a while ago, wasn't too far from here.

It was a little dark and a bit small, not exactly what I pictured for a restaurant, but that was how all the restaurants were in this part of town. In a city as old as this, space was very limited. "What do you think?" I turned back around to look at Axel.

He was wearing a long-sleeved gray shirt and black jeans, his thick muscles impervious to the cold. His hands were in his pockets, but he withdrew them and crossed his arms over his chest as he examined the bar. "A little small..."

"They're all this size on this street."

He stood at the counter and leaned forward. "You can only have about twelve tables at a time...and the kitchen is cramped."

"It's a starter restaurant. I'm not going to open an enormous place right off the bat."

"Why not?" He pivoted toward me as he leaned against the counter, the light from the hanging lamps striking his blue eyes perfectly. He was a beautiful man, and whenever we were out in public together, I noticed all the stares he got. I saw women ogle him openly, not caring whether I saw. There were times when it got under my skin, but I reminded myself it was the price I had to pay to have a gorgeous husband...and that was a fee I was happy to pay. When I didn't say anything, his eyes narrowed. "Baby?"

"Hmm?"

A slow grin moved over his face, like he suspected what had distracted me so deeply. "Why not start with a big restaurant?"

"Because I'd have to hire more staff to run it, which costs more money, and if I don't have customers to support that, then the business goes belly-up. Basically Business Management 101."

"You're preparing for failure before you've even named your restaurant."

"I'm not preparing for failure. Just being realistic."

"Look, I know everyone worth knowing in this city, and I know all the people who come to visit. I recommend your restaurant on opening night, they all love it, reviews come pouring in online and in the papers, and then your restaurant is a massive hit."

"It's only a massive hit if they like it."

"That is one thing we don't have to worry about," he said. "They'll love it."

"This is going to cost a lot of money," I said. "I don't want to lose it—"

"You won't."

"And I really don't want to lose your money—"

"*Our* money." He left the counter and straightened. "This place is too small, baby. Maybe for something casual like sandwiches and salads or a dessert shop, but not for your cooking. Your culinary excellence deserves serious fanfare. I see lots of black marble, coffered ceilings, gold tumblers, real fancy shit."

I rolled my eyes. "You're just used to fancy parties and snobby people."

"And I know what snobby people like—good food."

"I think I need a second opinion about the cooking. You seem like a guy who would be happy with a sandwich."

He grinned. "I have my own chef. So I'm used to the finer things in life."

"I still think you're biased."

"What does your father think?"

"I've never really cooked for him before. Sometimes I bring things by his house and he likes it, but I've never prepared a meal or anything."

"Invite him over for dinner and see what he thinks."

"Both of you together?" I asked in disbelief.

"He is my father-in-law."

"I don't know if I can trust him. I could put a pile of dog shit on his plate, and he'd eat it with a grin."

A slight chuckle escaped his lips. "I'd love to see that."

I smacked his arm playfully and turned to the door.

"You know who will give you their straight opinion?"

We walked out, and the real estate agent locked the door.

"I don't think this place is right for us," I said. "We'd like to keep looking." We said our goodbyes, and then Axel and I walked down the street, past the little shops, as we headed to our car a couple blocks away. "Who?"

"Theo."

I rolled my eyes. "You'll tell him to like it."

"I won't."

"And even if you don't, he's not going to insult his best friend's wife."

"He's not my best friend. He's my brother."

"Isn't that the same thing?"

"I'm not the kind of guy who has a best friend."

"What about me?" I asked. "I'm not your best friend?"

"You're definitely not in the friend zone, baby."

"You know what I mean."

"Trust me, I don't see you as a friend. Never have and never will."

I smirked slightly. "Well, I feel like in order to have a good relationship, you need to be friends. If that weren't true, then all we would do is fuck and do nothing else in between. We'd just sit there in silence."

"If it were up to me, we would be having more sex."

"What?" I asked incredulously. "We do it every morning and every night."

"And if you didn't get sore, there would be a lot more in between."

"Wow, I had no idea."

His hand reached to my ass and squeezed it, right in front of the people behind us. "With a pussy as pretty as yours, you shouldn't be surprised."

I smacked his arm away. "People are staring."

"I don't blame them." His arm moved around my waist, and he tugged me close into his side. "I'd be staring at your ass too."

"Not everyone is obsessed with my lady bits like you are."

"Oh, trust me." His lips moved to my ear. "They are."

---

Aldo escorted Theo into the kitchen. "What can I get you to drink?"

"He'll have what I'm having," Axel said.

Aldo nodded then poured him a scotch—on the rocks.

He left the room, and Theo took the spot next to Axel on the barstool as I cooked in the kitchen.

Theo clinked his glass against Axel's before he took a drink. "Never had a woman cook for me before."

"That's not true," I said as I turned back toward them to use the sink. "I made you those pistachio cannoli."

"Oh, that's right." Theo grinned at the memory. "They were good."

"Really? Because you didn't eat much of it."

"Well, I don't have a big sweet tooth."

When I looked at Axel, I stilled at the rage on his face. He normally wore a smile with a dash of arrogance in his eyes, but now he looked like he wanted to rip the faucet out of the sink and bash a hole in the wall. "I'm just teasing him—"

"Do me a favor and never bring that shit up again." Axel tilted his head back and drank his scotch in one go.

Theo smirked before he clapped him on the back. "It's all good, Axel. She got the guy she wanted."

Axel grabbed the bottle and refilled his glass, obviously still pissed.

Theo and I exchanged a quick look.

"What are you making?" he asked.

"A couple things." I listed off the entrees and the starters, a fusion of European flavors, some Mediterranean tastes with a bit of French cooking.

"That sounds good," Theo said. "I eat the same shit over and over. Will be nice to have something different."

Axel still didn't talk, more interested in the booze in his glass.

"Axel thinks I should open a restaurant, and I would love to have an honest opinion," I said. "He says his feedback is truthful, but I still wonder if he's a bit biased because I give him sex."

"Good sex," Axel added before he took another drink.

"Well, I'll give you my ruthless and honest opinion," Theo said. "Because I don't give a damn about offending anyone. If your food tastes like shit, I'll tell you."

"Thank you," I said.

Axel was still in a sour mood, but it started to lessen as time went on. The kitchen filled with the aromas of hot food, and my own stomach started to rumble. The hardest part about cooking was keeping everything hot and serving it all at once, but since Axel had a full chef's kitchen, I was able to manage it. "Alright, let's eat." I plated the food and brought out everything at once, the salad, the soup, and the main entrée.

Axel sat across from me, while Theo sat beside him. For the first few minutes, we ate in silence, utensils scraping against plates occasionally. I didn't ask Theo what he thought of the food, letting him give his own opinion when he was ready.

"I'm not a fan of lemon," Theo said. "And it's potent in this chicken."

"Okay, I used too much lemon." I made a note to myself.

"But damn, it's good," he said. "Nice texture. Cooked well but still juicy and tender. And what is in this?" He pointed to the orange sauce that went with it.

"Tarragon."

"Good shit." He continued to eat. "It's all good."

Axel grinned at me. "What did I tell you? This guy would not eat dog shit."

"What?" Theo asked quizzically.

"Nothing," Axel said quickly. "Don't worry about it."

"Who eats dog shit?" Theo asked.

"Dante," Axel said quickly.

"What?" he asked with a confused expression.

"Yep," Axel said before he took a drink. "Spread the word."

I shook my head. "I said my father would eat my cooking and smile even if it were dog shit. That's why I didn't ask for his opinion."

"I see," Theo said with a grin.

We ate in comfortable silence, the three of us devouring everything on our plates and washing it down with the wine and scotch.

"Axel thinks we should lease a big restaurant, but I think we should start off small," I said.

"Correction," Axel said. "She wants a hole-in-the-wall."

"Hole-in-the-wall places are always charming." I drank my wine, the only person at the table to have any.

"I don't think this food fits that aesthetic," Theo said. "This is the kind of food a billionaire eats with one of his many mistresses, so rich that his wife can't say anything. Otherwise, she'll lose her allowance for shopping sprees and trips with the girls."

Axel grinned because he was right. "Thank you."

"A place like that is awfully ambitious."

"I know the restaurant business," Theo said. "I think you'll be fine."

"That's right." I'd forgotten the times we visited his restaurant. We went there for our first date, and I'd enjoyed the food.

"I'm not a chef," Theo said. "But I know good food. This is good."

Axel stared at me. "Looks like it's two to one, baby."

"What have you got to lose?" Theo asked.

"Um, probably hundreds of thousands of euro..."

Theo shrugged. "No big deal."

"Maybe not for you." Rich people spent money like it meant nothing to them. My father was the same way, sometimes careless with his wealth, but never careless enough to give me a bigger piece of the pie.

"It's settled," Axel said. "We'll find a bigger place. Something more appropriate for this fine cuisine."

———

I brought the dishes and pans to the sink and started the faucet, letting the water run warm before soaking the sponge and squirting the soap in the center.

Axel stood across the counter from me. "What are you doing?"

My eyes lifted. "What does it look like I'm doing?"

"I have people for that."

"It's late, and it's not a big deal."

"They'll clean it tomorrow, then."

"I don't mind cleaning up after myself."

Axel came around the counter and shut off the faucet. "They had a night off because you did all the cooking. Think of it that way."

"I can carry my own weight around here." I turned on the faucet again.

He hit the handle and shut off the water. "If you do the cooking and the cleaning, then what do I need them for? You want them to lose their jobs?"

"No—"

"Then let's go to bed. Your food turns me on."

I released a chuckle. "Never heard that one before..."

"It's true. You're a master in the kitchen, and that's sexy. Like watching me work out is sexy."

"Are you a master in the weight room?"

His arm moved around my waist, and he flashed me that handsome grin. "Watch me and decide for yourself."

We left the kitchen and headed upstairs to the bedroom that felt like a mile away. The villa was grand, grand enough to be a boutique hotel that could accommodate twenty-five guests comfortably.

"You ever think about downsizing?" I asked when we walked into the bedroom.

"Why would I?"

"Because your bedroom is a five-minute walk from the main part of the house."

He entered the bedroom and tugged his shirt over his head, revealing a back hard with muscles that hugged both sides of his spine.

"I just think this place is too big for one person."

He kicked off his shoes and removed his jeans. "It's not one person. It's two." He faced me, standing in his black boxers, ripped and tight despite the heavy meal we'd just devoured. "And eventually, it'll be four. So I think it's just fine."

"Four?" I asked, eyebrows raised.

"You want more?"

"Are you referring to children?"

"Well, I'm not talking about dogs."

"I didn't realize you knew exactly how many kids you wanted."

"Women are the only ones allowed to think about that sort of thing?" He sat on the foot of the bed, knees wide apart, his hands together between his thighs.

"No...I just didn't think you did."

"I didn't enjoy being an only child. I think every kid deserves a sibling."

"Well, I was an only child, and I was fine with it."

"You only want one, then?"

"I'm not saying that—"

"Then how many do you want?"

"I—I don't know." I pulled my blouse over my head and tossed it on the armchair then moved to my jeans and shoes. I undressed in front of him, feeling his heavy stare glued to me. "I'm only twenty-five. Not really in a rush, I guess."

"I'm in my thirties now, so I'm in a different place." He watched me, his eyes hard. "But I'll be patient as long as you need me to."

"You'd want kids right now if I was willing?" I asked incredulously. "We've been married a couple months."

He gave a shrug. "Right this very second? Maybe not. But if we started trying in the next year...I wouldn't mind that."

"I'm not sure what to say to that. Normally, you've got to twist a guy's arm to get a ring and a family. They're too objective to understand the emotional fulfillment of children. All they focus on is the things they'll lose rather than the things they'll gain."

He gave a shrug. "If you asked me this a year ago, I'd probably agree with you."

"What changed?"

He continued to stare at me, that stare becoming hard as steel. He didn't speak, but he conveyed so much with that simple look.

I swallowed.

"Come here." He straightened and patted his thigh.

I moved to him, and instead of my sitting across his lap sideways, he pulled me onto him, adjusting me on his lap as his big hands squeezed my cheeks. He was so tall that we were still eye level even when I was on top of him, and those blue eyes made me weak all over.

He looked into my face like he'd never seen me before, never took the time to look at me. Then he touched his forehead to mine, his hands gripping my cheeks in my thong. His eyes dropped, looking down as he held me close.

My fingers moved into the back of his short hair, and I could feel the pulse in his neck with my fingertips. Soft. Slow. Soothing. An old pain ached in my heart, a pain that I'd shunted long ago. Being around him generated an energy that hurt as much as it felt good, a high that I'd never reached with anyone else. It happened every time I looked at him, every time I saw him smile, every time I felt him treat me like a goddess rather than yesterday's trash.

He lifted his gaze and locked on mine, his eyes somehow bright despite the darkness in the bedroom. He possessed his own luminance, a radiance that couldn't be shadowed by the heaviest rain cloud. After a quick glance at my lips, he leaned in and kissed me, a hard kiss that had no preamble. His mouth latched on to mine with intensity as his hand slid into my hair, fisting the strands and getting a hold of me like a rider with his horse. His other arm cradled me to him, keeping me secure on his lap as he kissed me like it was the first time he'd gotten the chance to feel my lips.

No one had ever kissed me with that kind of passion. No one had ever made me feel beautiful the way he did. He was the perfect man, on the inside as well as the outside, and it was easy to forget the way he'd hurt me.

Easy because I really believed he would never do it again.

Maybe that made me an idiot, but I didn't care.

He rolled me onto my back and moved on top of me, our bodies at the corner of the bed. His big hand grasped my thong and pulled it down until my legs were free of the silk. He tugged the front of his boxers down so his big dick could come free. Then we were united in a rush, his huge size filling me completely, our breaths coming out as muffled whispers.

He grabbed my ankle and positioned my foot against his chest, bending my flexible body like I was a doll, deepening the angle so he could make me feel the fullest I'd ever been. When I gave a wince at his intrusion, it only excited him. When he had me exactly where he wanted me, he grabbed me by the throat as he thrust into me, pounding into me with the power of a mountain.

I was possessed by this man, fully and utterly, and I'd never been possessed in the same way by anyone else. He marked me like a tattoo, branded me like a cow in his herd, tied an invisible leash around my throat that only the two of us could see.

"You're mine, baby." His fingers tightened on my throat a little more, almost cutting off my air.

His deep voice was like an addictive drug, so sexy it made me feel weak. My eyes closed, and I savored the way he spoke, locking it in the vault of my mind to treasure always.

"Say it."

My eyes opened again.

"Say it, baby."

"I'm yours..."

"Louder."

I tried to project my voice with his fingers firmly against my throat. I pushed through the pressure and let my voice sing. "I'm yours."

———

The valet tried to open the door for me, but Axel got there and shooed him away. "I got it." He opened the door and gave me his hand, helping me from the low seat to my feet. When we stepped onto the sidewalk, Axel tossed the valet the keys and then guided me to the entryway. There was a line of people, another party with champagne and gowns and tuxes.

"You ever get tired of these?" I asked him.

"Not when you're with me." His arm moved around my waist, and he pulled me close, pressing a kiss to the corner of my mouth.

We entered the villa, the grand entryway turned into a large party with waiters and a quartet filling the room with a symphony of music.

"Whose house is this?" I asked when the waiter handed us glasses of champagne.

"Arturo Balannie. He was the mayor of Florence for many years until he retired. My parents and I used to see him all the time."

"Will your parents be here?"

He shrugged. "Who knows?" He moved forward and spotted Arturo. "Happy birthday, Arturo. Not too many people live to be a hundred, so congratulations."

Arturo gave him a glare, but it was mixed with affection, the way a grandfather viewed his grandkids even when they were being rowdy and impolite. "My wife sure doesn't think I'm a hundred."

Axel gave him a wink before he nudged him in the side. "I like your style, man. Speaking of wives..." He turned to me. "This is Scarlett."

"I didn't know you were married." He shook my hand then kissed me on the cheek. "Lovely to meet you, dear."

"We got married a couple months ago," Axel said. "Kinda like a shotgun wedding but without the pregnancy."

"What was the rush?" Arturo asked.

"Look at her." Axel grinned. "When I got her to say yes, I didn't want to give her time to change her mind."

Arturo laughed, clearly smitten with Axel.

It was ridiculous because I knew every woman saw us together and wondered how I nabbed him. Tall, muscular, crystal-blue eyes...the guy had it all. And to top it off, he was so sweet. He seemed unreal at times, too good to be true. But somehow, he was mine—for the rest of my life, if that's what I wanted.

They talked for a while longer before we moved on so Arturo could chat with other people who'd come to his Tuscan villa to celebrate. It was freezing outside, winter lingering, but it was like a preheated oven indoors.

"He seemed nice," I said.

"Yeah, he's one of the good ones."

"Good ones?"

"Doesn't take bribes, have mistresses, that sort of thing."

"So if he knew the business you were in, would he want you here?"

"He knows."

"And he doesn't report you?"

"He's righteous, but he's not a rat." He finished his champagne with a grimace and set it on an empty tray carried by a passing waiter. "Hungry?"

"Sure."

We moved to an empty table, and Axel pulled out the chair for me. "I'll be back." He walked to the buffet line and took two plates, snagging a couple small appetizers before he returned. "I have no idea what any of this is, so I grabbed it all."

"Looks good." It was an assortment of small bites, brie backed in a delicate pastry, mini beef Wellingtons, and bacon-wrapped scallops.

His arm rested over the back of my chair, and he took a bite here and there but didn't seem hungry because he didn't scarf down his food like he normally did. "Not as good as your stuff."

"You don't have to compliment my food every time we eat."

"I mean it."

"But if you enjoy other food, it doesn't mean you're betraying me."

He smirked. "I could eat your food for every meal for the rest of my life. Same goes for your pussy."

I gave him a smack. "We're in public."

"So?" The grin remained. "No one heard me."

"You don't know that."

"And I don't care if they did."

"Well, I care." I dropped my voice to a whisper. "Don't want people to overhear us talking about my *girl*."

"Your girl?" he asked. "She's *my* girl."

"Don't be crude. We're at a party."

"You think that's crude? I'll take you into a guest bedroom and show you crude."

I smacked him in the arm. "My god."

His fingers touched my hair as he sat beside me, gently running through the strands. "I'm married to the woman of my dreams. Of course my dick is going to be hard all the time."

"Let's stop saying dick and pussy and everything else in between."

His smirk remained like he was having the time of his life. "What do you want me to say? I'm fucking happy." He glanced across the room, looked at the people as they mingled and drank, as they enjoyed the music.

I stared at the side of his face, his words sinking into me like pieces of metal. My heart tightened in my chest, giving a dull ache that interrupted my breathing. I could see the slight smile on his lips, see the joy in his eyes. Last time we'd gone to a party, his parents had been there, making their disownment very apparent. He was miserable. But now...he was a different man. "Why?"

"Come on, baby. Don't play dumb." He turned to look at me straight on. "You're the best thing that's ever happened to me." The slight smile on his lips slowly faded as he continued to look at my expression.

I didn't know how I looked, but I must have looked less than happy at that announcement. I felt trapped, restrained by invisible ropes that bound me in place, that prohibited me from being free. My heart wanted to sing and dance, to let him deep inside me, to know me the way he used to...but I just couldn't.

I couldn't.

It was a quiet ride home.

The elevator ride was stuffy.

The walk up the stairs and to the bedroom was somehow the most uncomfortable of all.

We entered the master suite, and I headed straight to the closet to slip off my heels and unzip the black dress. It was the first moment of privacy I'd had, the first moment I didn't have to share the contentious air with him.

I removed my jewelry and pulled on a shirt before I stepped out of the closet.

He sat in one of the armchairs, ankle crossed and resting on the opposite knee, his tie yanked loose with his jacket tossed over the back of the chair. He stared at me with that hard look, not the intense one that hinted at the desire beneath the surface, but the one that showed the depth of his anger, his disappointment.

I froze in place as if he'd just yelled at me when he didn't say a word. I stood there and waited for him to speak, to lash out at me, to say whatever was on his mind.

He propped his elbow on the armrest and dragged his fingers across his jawline. His blue eyes weren't bright anymore. No longer playful. Just dark and angry. "I can't do this anymore."

I sucked in a breath, feeling the same fist in my stomach as the night he'd left me.

"You're either in this marriage with me, one hundred percent, or you're not." He'd spoken at a normal decibel up until that point, but it skyrocketed after that. "Which is it?"

I stilled as if he'd just backhanded me.

"I'm tired of our moments being shattered by your sabotage. I'm tired of feeling you run whenever I get a little deeper into your heart. I'm tired of this fucking brick wall that you put up every time I get too close. This marriage is never going to work if you keep one foot out the door. Do you understand me?"

I was paralyzed by his anger. Paralyzed by the fact that he could read me so well, see my mind withdraw into another room when my body hadn't moved an inch.

He got to his feet, the top buttons of his shirt undone and revealing part of his chest. "Scarlett—"

"Yes, I understand you." I turned away.

"Then why aren't you looking at me?"

I focused on the window, which was obscured by the closed curtain. "It's not that easy...to just forget."

"It's not easy when you don't let yourself."

"That's not how the brain and the heart work. You have no idea how much you hurt me—"

"Yes, I do. I'm so sorry for what happened, but you need to forgive me and move on."

"Forgive you?" My eyes came back to him. "I never would have married you if I'd had another choice—"

"I said you could leave if you wanted, but you chose to stay."

"Well, maybe I shouldn't stay." My eyes flicked down, not wanting to look at his face. I had no idea how he looked, but I could feel the rush of pain fill the room like smoke. "As much as I...care for you...it's never going to go away."

"It's never going to go away if you don't let it go."

"Let it go?" I looked up to meet his stare. "If the situations were reversed, you would not let it go. You deserve a lot more than a woman who chooses someone else. You're too good and kind to settle for that."

He gave a sigh. "We can't have a marriage if you pull away every time we get close. I need you to let it go—for us."

"I don't think I can—"

"Yes, you can."

"*No.*" I looked away again, the roof of my mouth on fire from the impending tears. "It's really unfair that you pressure me to get over this when it wouldn't be easy for anyone to get over. You want us to be what we were, as if nothing happened, and that's just not possible. It would have been possible if you'd just—"

"I can't do this anymore. It's fucking bullshit, and I'm over it."

I stilled, feeling as if he'd slapped me again. "Thank you for being so understanding."

"That's not what I'm talking about." He took a couple breaths, his face tinted red in anger. "I trust you. I trust you with my fucking life. So I'm going to tell you something, and you have to promise me you'll keep it to yourself. Promise me."

My heart raced at a different speed as the situation became far more intense. As if I stood on the edge of a cliff, blind and deaf, I didn't know whether I should take a step back or a step forward. Any move was risky. "What—what do you need to tell me?"

"Promise you won't say a word of it to another soul—especially your father. Not only can you not tell him, but you have to act like there's nothing to tell, like everything is exactly the same between you. *Promise me.*"

My eyes flicked back and forth between his, my heart practically jumping out of my chest at this point. "You want me to keep a secret from him?"

"Yes."

"Will this secret cause anyone harm—"

"This secret has nothing to do with the present or the future. It's in the past. No one is at risk of harm. Well, except for me." He took a breath as he stared at me. "You may not believe me, but regardless, I need you to keep it to yourself. Can you do that?"

"If it's so risky, why even tell me—"

"Because I love you. And I'm not losing you. Not over this." He shook his head. "So, promise me."

A part of me wanted to wash my hands clean and walk away from this. I suspected this was something I was better off not knowing. But Axel's plea had me hooked to the spot. "Alright...I promise."

He dropped his chin and took a breath, both relieved and overwhelmed that I gave the answer he wanted. "Alright." He straightened, his eyes focused just a few inches below mine before he found the strength to look at me. "Remember when we pretended to break up to throw your father off the scent?"

"Yes."

"It worked. But when we went to that art gala, he caught me staring at you across the room." He grabbed his tie and pulled it from his neck altogether before he tossed it aside, missing the armchair because the material was so floppy. "It was just a look, but...it was enough. He told me I wasn't good enough for you and if I didn't leave you, there would be consequences."

I felt my chest expand to allow for bigger breaths. My pulse quickened, pounding in both my neck and my temple. The only thing I had in this world was my father, a man who loved me so much that he made every sacrifice with a smirk. I couldn't believe the accusation Axel was making. "What consequences?"

"He'd kill my father."

I took a step back, as if Axel had just threatened me. "No..."

"I tried to end things...you remember." His eyes dropped. "But you held on to me because you knew...you fucking knew that I didn't want to go. You believed in us so deeply, and it was fucking agonizing to try to shake you." He clenched his jaw. "Nothing has ever hurt so much in my damn life."

I shook my head, unable to believe it.

"One night, I went to see your father...and he had my father there...with a gun to his head. Said if I didn't do it, he would put him in the ground."

"No..."

His eyes lifted to mine. "I told him I loved you, and that I suspected you loved me, but that changed nothing." He shook his head. "Nothing at all. I told him I'd tried to shake you, but you wouldn't let me go...so he forced me to do something despicable." He swallowed. "Cassandra."

My arms folded over my chest as a protective barrier, but they couldn't protect my heart from his words.

"He shot my father in the arm anyway, just because I'd taken so long."

I pulled my gaze away from his face entirely, the adrenaline pumping through my heart so potent that I started to feel dizzy. My fingers squeezed my arms like a crutch, but I was too weak to support my body. I opened my mouth to speak, but hardly anything came out. "No..."

"I wouldn't lie to you."

I wouldn't look at him. "My father would never..." I shook my head because I just couldn't believe it. "He would never do something like that."

"Baby."

My eyes were determined to avoid his.

"You know I wouldn't lie to you about something like this. I wouldn't lie to you about anything."

"My dad wouldn't hurt an innocent person—"

"*He did.*" Now his voice was no longer gentle, but callous. "What little hope I had left that my parents and I would reconcile disappeared that night. My parents barely tolerated my presence before, but now they refuse to be in the same room with me. My father's arm will be fucked up for the rest of his life, and he blames me for that...as he should. But I still walked away from the love of my life to keep him alive. I let her think that I would replace her with someone else as if she meant nothing to me...just to keep him alive. Keep alive a man who despises me."

I stared at the floor, trembling. "I..." I didn't know what to say. Where to start. What to believe.

"He said I wasn't good enough for you. That I'm some barbaric criminal. But I think that was all an excuse. He just wanted to use you to further his gains, and setting you up with the Skull King was the perfect union. If Theo and I weren't close, your father would have forged an alliance with the most powerful kingpin in Italy. Just like the princesses who were married to princes of other powerful kingdoms...all to increase their territory and power. He says I'm barbaric, but he treats you like a fucking bargaining chip."

"My father loves me—"

"I know he does. But he uses you too."

I stepped away, turned my back to Axel, and moved closer to the wall. There was a painting there I'd never noticed before. I stared at it without really seeing it, my hands continuing to squeeze my arms.

He gave me a couple minutes to absorb all the horror.

I continued to stare at the painting.

"Think about it," he said quietly. "What are the odds that I would walk into the same restaurant as you with another woman?"

My breathing remained hard. My eyes turned wet.

"Quite a coincidence, if you ask me."

I stared at the floor next.

His voice dropped. "It ruined me to do that to you."

The memory was still horrible, seeing him pull out the chair for her and drink his wine.

"I begged him not to make me do it—fucking begged—but he didn't give a shit. As long as he got what he wanted, he didn't care about the consequences. He didn't care that it broke your heart irrevocably." He came closer to me, his voice growing louder. "Screwing over your father and demanding you to be my wife was the only way I could get you back. It's not how I wanted to do things. It's not how I wanted us to have our wedding. But I think we would have ended up together if your father hadn't manipulated us both. I believe we would have ended up together." His hands moved to my shoulders, and he gripped me, his head resting against the back of my head. "Baby?"

I stepped away, needing air to breathe, needing to escape the suffocating heat that had come out of nowhere.

He gave a sigh in disappointment.

"He—he wouldn't do that to me." I faced him again, tears heavy in my eyes.

"I know this is a lot—"

"He would never..." The tears grew so heavy, they skidded down my cheeks.

"I know this is a lot," he repeated. "But I wouldn't lie to you."

"And my father would never do something so heinous—"

"It comes down to this." He came closer to me. "One of us is lying—and it's not me."

"You could have made all of this up so I would forget about Cassandra."

He gave an annoyed sigh. "Quite an elaborate lie."

I stepped away, needing more space from him.

He winced when I moved away from him. "I'm not lying, Scarlett."

"Then let me confront my father—"

"No. I told you what he'll do."

"But if he tries to kill your father, I'll know it's him—"

"And he said if that happens, he'll lose you, so I may as well lose someone too." He came closer to me. "You promised me you wouldn't say anything. My father's life is literally on the line right now."

"It's an amazing coincidence that you're accusing my father of all these things, and I can never question him about it." My eyes shifted away. "That he can never confirm or deny these allegations. Quite convenient." My eyes moved back to him.

He wore an expression he'd never had before. The anger in his eyes was masked with defeat. His shoulders slouched. His skin was suddenly paler than it'd ever been. All the intensity he usually wore when he looked at me had evaporated in just a few seconds. "You don't believe me."

"I—I didn't say that."

"You either believe me, or you don't," he said simply. "I thought you would."

"My father... We're so close. He loves me so much. I just can't—"

"I love you more than he ever will. Than he ever has." He continued to speak with defeat, without passion. "When I tried to break things off and you wouldn't let me, I fell so fucking hard for you. When you asked if there was something I wasn't telling you, I wanted to break down. You saw me in a way no one ever has. I hoped that telling you the truth would bring that back, would make you look at me like that again. But I can see that it hasn't." He crossed his arms over his chest and stared at the floor. "You either need to forgive me for what you think happened with Cassandra...or you need to believe my story. If your answer is neither, I think this marriage is over." He lifted his eyes to look at me, the sorrow heavy in his stare, like he already knew what I would say. "I love you...so fucking much, but I can't keep fighting for you. I can't continue to fight a battle that I clearly have no chance of winning."

Tears streaked down my cheeks, a culmination of all my emotions, all my despair. The sobs wanted to rack my chest, but I kept them back, refusing to dissolve into a puddle right before his eyes.

He stared at me for minutes and waited for me to say something, his eyes still hollow, still devoid of all emotion. Then he cleared his throat. "It's late." He rubbed one of his arms through the sleeve of his shirt. "I'll sleep in the guest room tonight. Aldo will help you with your things in the morning." His words trailed off like there could be more, like he hoped I would interrupt him, tell him that I wanted to stay, that I believed his story...

But I didn't.

# Chapter 5

## *Scarlett*

I sat at the kitchen table with a hot cup of coffee in front of me, the steam wafting from the dark surface and hitting me in the face. The days had started to get longer now that we were closer to spring, but the cold was still rampant, the draft felt every time I came too close to the window when I passed.

My old apartment was exactly as I remembered it. To my good fortune, no one had rented it in the brief time I'd lived with Axel. His men took all my clothing and belongings and delivered them, along with me, to this place.

Now I sat there alone, lower than I'd ever been in my life.

There were times when I wanted to go back to Axel because I missed him so much, but then the past would loom over us like a bad dream. I would think of the way he'd treated Cassandra so delicately...the way he treated me. Or I would think about the horrible accusation he'd made, that my own flesh and blood would betray me like my worst enemy. Either way, our relationship was doomed to die. We were like a newly potted plant. It looked nice for a few days, but then the dead soil or the lack of sunshine killed it. The plant was replaced, only to have the same outcome.

I continued to stare at my coffee but never took a sip. Sometimes the steam distracted me, blanketed my face with moist heat that made my cheeks feel wet...without any tears.

I'd left my ring on his nightstand before I moved out. My finger felt naked now. The weightlessness was freeing, but not in the good kind of way, more in the falling off a building toward the pavement kind of way.

My heart ached with a hole that would never heal. The memory of his smirk and his playful eyes would haunt me forever. He made me feel so warm, even in the darkest hour. When I had been about to lose my life, he was there to save me. He saved my father too, and if his accusation about him were true, then that would have been a noble act.

Three days had passed, and I still didn't know what to think.

Axel hadn't texted or called.

And I knew he wouldn't.

---

I sat on the couch in the parlor, my eyes glued to the dancing flames in the hearth. Gas fireplaces were more convenient and pollutant-free, but there was something special about a real fire, the way the flames made the wood crackle and pop. It was mesmerizing, and like the steam from my coffee, it distracted me...for a brief moment.

"Sweetheart." My father rounded the corner, entering the room with his welcoming posture, his handsome smile, but it took only two seconds for his mood to dim and mirror mine. "Everything alright?" He came to the couch and stood over me for a moment, his eyes jumping back and forth to take in my ghost-white face.

"Yes, everything's fine." My voice didn't sound like my own, sounded like it belonged to a stranger.

My father slowly lowered himself to the couch across from me, his concerned eyes locked on me with such anguish. His spine didn't touch the back of the couch, prepared to launch toward me if I collapsed on the floor. He continued to stare. "Sweetheart, you look..." He hesitated, replacing whatever he was about to say with something more polite. "You look unwell."

I showered every day because I couldn't stand oily hair, but I put no effort into my appearance. Instead of giving myself a blowout for shiny and silky hair, I let it air-dry. As a result, I had a disheveled appearance. I didn't bother with makeup, so my face was washed out, my features all blending together in an unremarkable look. "I came by because I wanted to talk to you about something."

"I'm listening," he said quickly, anxious to hear the source of my misery.

"I want to ask you something..." My eyes dropped down to the table between us, the pain in my chest so unbearable it was hard to make eye contact. I knew Axel's character, and he wasn't the kind of man to lie. He was the kindest, most generous man I'd ever met. Despite the end of our marriage, I was lucky I'd ever gotten to be with him. But my father was also a wonderful man, and I couldn't see him doing the heinous things Axel accused him of. It was hard to believe either of them would ever hurt me, but someone had.

"Alright," my father said, eager for me to continue.

My eyes remained on the table, wanting to believe in my heart that my father was innocent of Axel's allegations, that he wouldn't threaten an innocent person, that he wouldn't shoot someone in the arm just to make a point. I needed to hear him deny all of this, to tell me it was ridiculous even to entertain it for a couple seconds.

"Sweetheart?"

My eyes lifted to meet his. I stared at his hard features, the jawline that cast a shadow under his chin, the stubble that he'd let grow for a couple of days. His eyes were soft when it was just the two of us, but I'd seen their softness harden into the point of a dagger in the company of others.

He couldn't have done it...he just couldn't.

His eyes narrowed in impatience.

I knew my father didn't do it, and if I asked him, that's what he would say. Axel's father wasn't in danger. It was just an elaborate lie.

But what if I was wrong?

What if—what if it was true?

"I was wondering...if you would give me a loan to open my restaurant." My eyes lifted to meet his, a flush of adrenaline rushing through me and dissipating just as quickly as it started. I swallowed again.

It took him several long seconds to process that request. "That's what you wanted to discuss?"

"Yes."

A heavy sigh escaped his nostrils, like he'd been prepared for much worse news. "Did something happen with Axel?"

I swallowed, so paralyzed I wasn't sure if I could say the words.

He seemed to understand because he gave a slight nod. "I'm sorry, sweetheart." He said it in a delicate voice, like he meant every word he said, like he was saddened by my heartbreak. "May I ask what happened?"

I crossed my legs then gripped my knee with both hands. I stared at my locked fingers, listening to the fire crackle in the background. "I tried to forget about what happened with Cassandra, but I just couldn't." My eyes lifted to see his reaction.

His expression hadn't changed. It was focused and intense, his eyes serious. Then he gave a slight nod. "Under-standable."

I continued to stare, to pierce his expression with the sharpness of my eyes, to see any indication of a lie. If he was guilty of what Axel said, it didn't seem like it. Or was he just the best liar in the world, should compete in poker tournaments and clean house? The only things I saw on his handsome face were sorrow and concern and devastation.

He stared at me for a while, his sadness continuing to match mine.

"I moved back to my old apartment a few days ago."

He continued to stare. "Instead of pursuing a restaurant, how about you return to the family business?"

I used to be so ambitious, but now the suggestion was repulsive. "I never want to return to the family business."

His disappointment was so heavy it couldn't be masked. "Sweetheart, I assure you what happened was an unusual occurrence—"

"I'm too soft for that kind of life."

His voice deepened. "You are not soft, Scarlett."

If Axel hadn't shown up, I would have been raped and killed. The threat was enough to give me nightmares for the rest of my life. "I don't want it. I'm sorry."

His eyes dropped for the first time.

I felt bad for disappointing him. I always tried to please him, always tried to make him proud, but this was something I was unwilling to do. No amount of guilt would change my mind.

He looked away, staring at the fire for a while.

I didn't ask about the loan again, because truthfully, I didn't want it. I'd just needed something to say in that heated moment. I would go to the bank and do it the traditional way, the way everyone who didn't have rich fathers and husbands did.

He remained quiet, lost in his own thoughts and his sea of disappointment.

I noticed he didn't ask how I was doing. If I needed anything. If there was anything he could do to ease my pain. He seemed to be thinking about himself, the fact that my separation from Axel had complicated his ownership.

That stung a bit. "I should go." I rose to my feet and grabbed my purse.

After a second, he did the same and came to my side. "How much do you need?"

"I—I don't know. Maybe a hundred thousand."

He walked with me toward the door, his hands in his pockets. "I'll think about it and let you know."

I didn't want the loan, but it hurt that he didn't give it to me without hesitation. Axel was happy to give me everything of his, to push his wealth into my hands for me to keep. He was happy to make my dreams a reality. Both men were equally wealthy, so it was clear who was generous...and who was stingy. "Alright. Goodnight."

He opened the front door for me. "Sweetheart?"

"Hmm?" I turned back to look at him.

"Don't be sad for long," he said. "You were too good for him anyway."

# Chapter 6

## *Axel*

Aldo knocked on my bedroom door.

I was on the couch in the living room, watching a game I didn't really care about. Sports was the only distraction I had at the moment. All of her stuff was gone, but her smell remained. Hints of her perfume in the bathroom. A pair of her panties in my underwear drawer that had been placed there by mistake. One of her hairs on my pillow. Everywhere I looked, she was there, fucking haunting me.

Aldo knocked again, like he knew I was there and ignoring him. "Sir, Theo is here to see you."

Why? "Tell him I'm not home."

"I've already informed him you're in residence."

My eyebrow cocked at his boldness as I walked to the door, tired of talking through a wall. "Why would you do such a thing?"

He stepped back from the door and placed his hands behind his back. "He's waiting for you in the parlor."

"You already invited him into the house?" I asked incredulously.

Aldo walked off, like this was acceptable behavior for a butler.

I growled before I slammed the door behind me. I was in nothing but my boxers, so I pulled on a pair of sweats and a shirt before I took the long trek down the stairs and into the parlor on the lower level.

Theo was already there, but the decanter of scotch was untouched, and so were the cigars.

*Something was up.*

When I walked into the room, his eyes immediately locked on my appearance, like he was looking for bullet wounds or scars.

It took only a few seconds to piece together what had happened. Aldo had betrayed me. That man was supposed to be my secret keeper. If I killed someone in the house and he was questioned by authorities, he was supposed to keep his mouth shut. "That little traitor..." I sat in the armchair across from Theo, the window behind me.

Theo massaged his knuckles as he stared at me, as if he'd recently got into a fistfight in a bar. "He hadn't seen you in three days...started to get worried."

I looked at the fire, not in the mood to talk to anyone, not even him. The last three days had been spent on the couch. Hardly ate anything. Skipped the gym every single day, which was a new streak for me. I simply had no motivation to do anything. Every time I looked at my phone, I hoped to see a message from her...but there was nothing.

"You want to talk about it?"

"Does it look like I want to talk about it?" My eyes stayed on the fire.

Theo leaned forward and helped himself to one of the cigars on the tray.

I wasn't in the mood for a smoke. I wasn't even in the mood for booze.

"I'm sorry, Axel."

That didn't make me feel better whatsoever.

We sat there for a long time, just absorbing the mutual silence. Theo continued to enjoy his cigar, and I continued to stare at the fire like he wasn't there. Whenever I looked at the flames, I was reminded of Scarlett's passion, of the way her fire leaped when I added my gasoline.

"Have you spoken to her?"

"No."

"She'll come back."

"She won't." I turned to look at him. "I told her the truth about Dante."

The cigar no longer seemed important because he kept it between his fingers rather than between his lips.

"She didn't believe me."

Anger flashed across his eyes, subtle but significant. "You think she'll confront him?"

"She promised she wouldn't."

"And you believe that?"

I nodded. "I wouldn't have told her if I didn't."

"Your father's life is literally in her hands right now."

"And that trust is well-placed." She thought so little of me, but I thought the world of her. I knew she would never betray me, whether we were together or not. She had a good heart, and unfortunately, I wasn't the only one to see that. Her father did too—and he chose to abuse it.

Theo stared at me for a while but didn't press his disagreement.

"I love her, but I couldn't do it anymore. We'd have a special moment that would only last a couple seconds before she got this look in her eyes...like our happiness only reminded her of her misery. In the blink of an eye, she'd remember my betrayal, and then the divide between us was even bigger than the previous one."

"One step forward, three steps backward."

"Exactly. I gave her an ultimatum. Forgive me—or forget me." And she chose wrong.

Theo stared at me, clearly at a loss for words. He'd never been one for deep conversation or a discussion about his feelings, so his silence was unsurprising. His presence was his love language.

I reached for a cigar and lit up.

"Just kill him, Axel."

"And what will that do?"

"He deserves it."

"I already lost her, so his death won't benefit me, just hurt her."

"I think it'll benefit her in the long run."

It did bother me that her father was the puppet master and she was the one on strings. She assumed she had a guardian angel looking after her, but she was just a pawn in his chess game. She had no free will, despite what she thought. When I told her I loved her more than he did, that was the truth.

"Then what are you going to do?"

"What do you mean? It's done."

"It's not done," he said. "You've been obsessed with this woman since the moment you saw her."

I knew I would never get over her. Not really. She would always be the one who got away. Time would pass, and I would think of her less and less. I'd meet someone else at some point, and it would feel right. But in the back of my mind, she would always be there, a permanent mark that had become a part of me. And if I bumped into her on the street, all those feelings would rush back...and I would play an extensive game of what-if. It would be hard to shake the memory, and when I was in bed with my woman, she would pop in here and there. It would be a shitty feeling, to want to move on but be forever stuck in the past. "I deserve to be with a woman who wants me fully. Not partially. Not begrudgingly."

"It was never begrudgingly, man."

"She's not here, is she?"

The cigar continued to burn unattended in his fingertips. "She made the wrong decision, but I understand the complexity of her situation. Nobody could fathom their own father lying straight to their face like that. That the person they trust most is not the person they thought they were. If she can't confront him about it, what else is she supposed to do?"

I stared at the cigar in my fingertips and watched it burn.

"You know I'm right."

I continued to stare.

"You should talk to Dante."

My eyes flicked up. "And what will that do?"

"He'd be dead right now if it weren't for you. He owes you."

"He's never going to throw himself under the bus—"

"Convince him. Tell him you'll mend the relationship between him and Scarlett."

"He'll never go for it."

"You want this woman or not?" He cocked his head to the side.

"I do, but I'm tired of fighting for her."

"This goes beyond you and her. You're fighting for her freedom because she has no idea she's being oppressed by this psychopath. Every relationship she has after you will be manipulated by this guy. She could end up with an asshole simply because he's beneficial to Dante. Something to think about."

The misery struck me like a bell tolling at the church. She'd left me, but I was still responsible for her well-being and her happiness. It felt like a curse, to love a woman who was impossible to love.

"Or, like I said, you could just kill him..."

I closed my eyes at the suggestion.

"I could do it for you. Keep your hands clean."

My eyes opened again. "As tempting as that is, I couldn't do that to her."

"You would be doing her a favor."

"It wouldn't feel like a favor to her."

"Then you need to expose him. That's your only option."

I would never get Dante to agree to the truth, to come clean and shed his skin. But I had to try...for her.

"Not to sound like an insensitive prick, but the Colombians have come back to the table."

At the change of subject, I returned the cigar to my mouth and let the smoke coat my tongue. "Really?"

He nodded. "Looks like they've had a change of heart."

"Did they agree to their original fee?"

"We haven't discussed details. They just said they want to meet."

"Ambush?"

Theo shrugged. "I doubt it. They probably realized they're sitting on a ton of product they can't move."

"Should we say we've already found another supplier?"

"Yes. Bring them back to their original fee. Dante won't like it, but he's a fucking pussy."

"And he's outnumbered two to one."

"Exactly. I'll set up the meeting."

"Alright." I wasn't as invested as I normally would be. Whether this deal worked out or not, I'd lost the one thing I actually cared about.

I stood in the parlor near the fire and waited for Dante.

It was the first time I'd left the house since Scarlett had moved back to her old apartment. Now that she was gone, the city looked different. The lights that shone on the Duomo weren't as bright. The starlight was obscured by clouds. The most romantic city in the world had become the dullest. I'd never considered myself a romantic guy, but I'd turned into Romeo when I'd met my Juliet.

When his footsteps sounded, I turned from the fire to meet his gaze.

His look was guarded and cold, like it wasn't the least bit pleasing to meet me tonight. Perhaps he already knew Scarlett and I had separated. Perhaps he didn't. Since I hadn't spoken to Scarlett, I really had no idea how she lived her life without me.

He moved to the couch and sat down, one ankle on the opposite knee, his stare hostile.

I crossed the room and sat across from him.

There was a showdown between us, an exchange of ruthless stares.

He was the first to speak. "Why are you here?"

"Your daughter left me."

There was no surprise. There was no remorse either.

"Said she couldn't move past my infidelity."

The guy didn't even blink.

"If you don't feel any ounce of guilt, then you must really be a psychopath."

"Or I just don't like you."

*Asshole.* "The only feelings that matter are your daughter's. She's making a decision without the facts, a decision that will affect the rest of her life. Tell her the truth so she can stop being miserable."

"Miserable?" he asked. "She seemed fine to me."

An explosion of pain hit my chest, the devastation passing in aftershocks.

"She said she was relieved it was over for good." He said it with a straight face, like a weatherman reporting the weather during the nightly news.

For an instant, I succumbed to it, picturing her happy while I was miserable on the couch all day. So miserable that I'd barely eaten since the morning she'd walked out. "You can't manipulate me the way you manipulate Scarlett. I know how much she's hurting right now. And she knows how much I'm hurting."

Dante didn't deny the accusation, but he kept a straight face like a poker champion.

"I love your daughter, Dante. I would die for her. I would give her my lungs if she couldn't breathe. I would give her my heart if hers stopped beating. You may not like me, but you know that I'm good for her."

He continued his hostile stare.

"Despite our differences, I'm not interested in sabotaging your relationship the way you're interested in sabotaging mine. I understand what you mean to her, and I would never undermine that. Let's move forward and make this work."

"I don't understand your meaning, Axel."

"I want your daughter—so name your price."

His arms crossed over his chest, and he took several seconds to process my statement. "I can't convince her to come back to you, Axel."

"You can if you tell her the truth."

The arrogance in his eyes suddenly faded, provoked by the scandalous suggestion.

"Name your price."

"There is no price, Axel. I'll take it to the grave."

"I love your daughter, and she loves me—"

"I've never heard her say such a thing—"

"You don't need to hear someone say it to know how they feel. It's in her stare. It's in the way she asks me to let her know that I'm okay. It's in the way she grabs my hand under the table. It's in everything she does. But she's too afraid to say it because of the way I hurt her. The way *you* made me hurt her."

Dante kept his arms across his chest.

"All I want is her. Please."

After a pause, he shook his head slightly. "No."

"Tell her the truth, and I promise I'll get her to forgive you. I will mend the relationship, and we can move forward."

"Even if that's true, it'll never be the same—"

"Our lives will never be the same if we aren't together." I spoke calmly, with a note of defeat, because I didn't expect this to succeed. But I tried anyway. "I love her so damn much. She loves me. It'll be a tragedy if we don't end up together because you intervened. A fucking tragedy. How does that not bother you?"

"Because my daughter is smart and beautiful and can have any man she wants. She'll be just fine without you."

"But I'm the man she wants, Dante. And you aren't letting her have what she wants."

"I'm not doing anything. She's the one who's choosing to leave—"

"*Because of you.* Make this right. If you love your daughter, you'll make this right."

"And if I could do that without compromising our relationship, I would. But that's not possible. She's the single most important thing to me. I would never jeopardize that."

"But you did jeopardize it with your lies."

"I was trying to protect her—"

"From the best thing that ever happened to her?" I asked incredulously. "I treat her like a fucking goddess, Dante."

"Did you treat your last wife like a goddess?" he asked coldly.

"I know you don't believe that."

"I believe in facts, Axel. And you went to prison for two years—"

"It's not true. And your daughter knows it's not." I raised my hand. "I'm tired of having this same conversation—"

"As am I," he snapped.

"I'm willing to leave the past behind us. I'm willing to give you a clean slate. I'm willing to try to accept you as my father-in-law. I will fight for your relationship with Scarlett. By telling her the truth, you'll have redeemed yourself in my eyes as well as hers. I'll give you back your business. I'll do anything you want at this point. Just tell her the truth. You can tell whatever convoluted version of the story you want. I just want her to understand that I did not end things because I wanted to. I did not go out with Cassandra because I wanted to. Please, Dante."

He listened to my speech with a blank stare, like he hadn't heard a word I said. He rubbed his arm and released a breath from his nostrils. "I can't help you, Axel. I suggest you move on and forget my daughter—just as she'll forget about you."

# Chapter 7

## *Scarlett*

Instead of waiting for my father to decide to give me the loan, I went to the bank and applied for one myself. I qualified for just enough to get a small place near Pino's. I decided to go back to the place that Axel and I had first visited, the one he'd described as a hole-in-the-wall.

I signed the lease agreement then got to work, spending hours in my apartment creating recipes that I would serve. My time was spent traveling back and forth between my apartment and the market, picking up more groceries to prepare meals in my kitchen. My days were packed from dawn to midnight, cooking or speaking with vendors who could supply all the products I needed to operate the restaurant. I didn't even have a name for it yet, but I had created nearly the entire menu by the end of the week.

I wasn't sure if I was excited for the restaurant or just desperate to stay busy. With a packed schedule, I barely had time to reflect on anything, so that meant I hardly thought of Axel, which was exactly what I wanted. Instead of wondering what he was doing or if he was watching the game, I was too busy cooking or washing the grease off my dirty pans. Instead of wondering if he was already sleeping around, I was asleep the moment my head hit the pillow.

I'd just finished another concoction when someone knocked on my door.

I turned off all the burners and felt my heart lunge, secretly hoping that it was Axel on the other side of that door, that he'd come to check on me, to tell me he was as miserable as I was.

But I knew it wasn't him.

It'd been over a week since I'd left, and he hadn't texted me. Hadn't called. It wouldn't make sense for him to show up on my doorstep unannounced. And even if he did... nothing had changed. It would only hurt us both.

"Sweetheart?"

My heart deflated at the sound of my father's voice. The disappointment caught me off guard. I walked across the apartment and opened the door to see him standing on the other side, looking nice in his blazer and collared shirt.

"Hey, Dad." I let him inside and didn't hug him like I normally would. Not only was I dirty in my apron, but I also didn't have the heart for human affection right now. Axel was the last person to have touched me. "What brings you here?"

"Just wanted to check on you. Haven't heard from you in a while." He eyed the mess in the kitchen.

"Just been busy."

"Something smells good."

"I'm working on recipes for the restaurant."

"Oh really?" He entered the kitchen and took a look inside the pans. "What's this?"

"Short rib ravioli. A long process to prepare the meat and then roll it in the ravioli, but it's worth it. I think it'll be a customer favorite when the restaurant opens."

"Can I try it?"

"Oh, sure." I took out a couple plates from the cabinet and dished up the ravioli before I placed the dishes on the kitchen table. The pans were left on the stove to be cleaned later. I opened a bottle of wine too and poured two glasses.

I hadn't sat down to eat since I'd left Axel's. I snacked here and there whenever I cooked because I didn't have much of an appetite. It was hard to believe I could lose weight in such a short amount of time, but I could tell my sweatpants fit differently.

My father took a bite, took his time chewing it, and then gave a nod. "Delicious."

"You really think so?"

"I do." He stabbed another ravioli and took a bite.

"You know there's carbs in that, right?"

He smirked as he chewed. "Worth it."

I looked down at my food and pushed the raviolis around. I had a small appetite, but it suddenly vanished into thin air like I'd never been hungry at all. The food was piping hot and imbued with my effort, but that still wasn't enough enticement.

My father watched me, his stare interrupted when he took a bite of his food. Silverware clanked against the plates, the sound a replacement for our usual conversation. The blinds on the windows were closed, but it was obvious that it was pitch dark outside.

He interrupted the silence with a question. "How are you?"

My eyes remained down on my food, looking at the cream sauce I'd made from scratch. "Fine." Now that I was seated at the table without a preoccupation, I was left to think about the man I'd lost. Was he home right now? Or was he out on the town, forgetting me?

He stopped eating his dinner even though he'd only eaten half of it. Maybe he didn't really like it. Or maybe his obsession with his body-fat percentage was more important. I noticed that trait in the men from this world, the desperation to be as trim and strong as possible, like it made them more intimidating. Axel wasn't intimidating... just sexy. "It's been a week since I've seen you. I expected you to feel better."

"Sorry to disappoint you," I said with my head down.

"You're the one who chose to leave, sweetheart."

"Trust me, it's not because I wanted to." I finally lifted my chin and set down my fork, tired of poking at my food like I was panning for gold.

He watched me, his hands together on his lap, legs crossed.

I looked out the window, feeling the hot burn of tears behind my eyes. The last thing I wanted to do was cry in front of my father, to let him see me cry over a man who'd dumped me for someone else, but I didn't have a mother to embrace me with open arms, to let me cry on her shoulder as she rubbed my back. My father and I were close, but we didn't talk about this sort of thing. I took a couple breaths to steady my emotions, but I felt the moisture creep toward the backs of my eyes like an incoming tide. "He's the love of my life." I felt my bottom lip tremble when I said those words, and it took several seconds to steady it before I continued. I looked so ugly when I cried, and I didn't want my father to see that. I only wanted him to know the poised version of me, the strong version of me. "I'll never love anyone the way I love him. But...I just can't get past it."

His eyes immediately dropped, probably because he didn't want to watch the tears break loose and streak down my face.

"He makes me so happy, and everything feels so right...but then the memory creeps in. The way he walked past our table. The way he pulled out the chair for her. The way he poured her a glass of wine before he filled his own. The way she blatantly flirted with him right in front of me at that party...and then he fucked her." I felt the tears break through, rivers down my cheeks that met the shores of my lips. "The way he replaced me...just like that." I breathed for several seconds, forcing myself to calm down so the tears would dry before I continued to speak.

His eyes remained locked on the table.

"And I didn't hear from him again. Like he forgot about me..." An apology from him wasn't enough. A declaration of his fidelity wasn't enough, even though I believed he would keep that promise. "I know this makes me sound like a stupid woman, but I believe he wouldn't hurt me again. He told me he loves me, and I believe him. But it's just not enough." I reached for the linen and dabbed my face, wiping the old tears from my cheeks.

He was still as a statue, visibly uncomfortable, his jaw clenched slightly.

Ashamed of my weakness, I looked between the partially open blinds over the window and stared at the lights that peeked through. If I could erase the last five minutes of the conversation, I would. But it was done.

After a long pause, he broke the silence. "I didn't know you felt that way."

I slowly turned back to him. "We don't really talk about this sort of thing."

His eyes lifted to meet mine. "His past doesn't bother you? I think that's a bigger issue than the infidelity."

"It's not true."

"What makes you so sure?"

"I..." I didn't have evidence. I only had his word. "Because I know him. He would never..." I shook my head. "There was never a time in our relationship when I felt unsafe or manipulated. He's—he's the best."

My father gave a slight nod. "I'm not one to give relation-ship advice since I've never really been in one, but it sounds like..." He hesitated, taking a slow breath and letting it go. "It sounds like he's an upstanding man who just made a mistake. If you love this man and believe in his reformed integrity, you should make it work. Remember that you're already married, you've already committed, so it's worth the effort."

His words surprised me enough to lull me into seconds of silence. "I thought you said he wasn't good enough for me."

"What I think doesn't matter, sweetheart."

"You've always told me I deserve a man who will give me the world. If he cheated on me, how could you encourage me to pursue the relationship? I only married him because I had to. If I'd had a choice in the matter, it never would have happened."

He rested one arm on the table and stared at it for a while. The silence lasted so long, it seemed like he hadn't heard everything I'd just said. Then he finally lifted his strong gaze and looked at me. "Axel and I haven't always gotten along, but I can't deny the depth of his feelings for you. The feelings you expressed to me...are very much reciprocated. While I don't condone what happened in the past..." He paused, dropping his gaze back to his arm for a few seconds before he looked at me again. "I do believe that love deserves a second chance. Real love doesn't come easy, and if you really have it, don't let it go."

His words left me speechless. He wasn't a romantic guy who rooted for relationships. He saw the world in black and white, right and wrong, and based on my feelings, he would normally knock Axel's teeth out. But he'd said something else entirely, something that dug deep under my skin and spread.

He cleared his throat, his declaration of a subject change. "I've decided to grant you the loan for the restaurant. I think it'll be nice for you to have something that's just yours."

"Oh...I already got a loan from the bank."

"Why?" His voice changed, hardening like our previous emotional conversation hadn't just taken place.

I shrugged. "I guess I didn't want to wait."

"Sweetheart, I just needed to think about it—"

"But I don't want your money if you have to think about it." I didn't mean to snap, not when he was so good to me and did offer me the money, but my temper was running rampant these last ten days.

He stilled at the ire in my voice and withdrew his arm from the table. "My hesitation was not a reflection of my belief in your success."

"Then what was the hesitation?" I put him on the spot and backed him into the corner with my eyes.

He stared me down in silence, holding my gaze like an enemy rather than family. "I guess it's hard for me to accept that you've chosen to leave the family business. That's my problem, not yours."

"So you use your money to leverage me?"

"Where is this hostility coming from?" He raised his voice, only slightly, and he hadn't done that since I was still living under his roof. "I didn't offer you the money instantly, but I'm offering it to you now."

"Well, I already got the loan from the bank, so this conversation doesn't matter."

"The interest on those loans is ridiculous. Take the money and pay off the loan."

"I'm good."

His eyes narrowed, and I knew his anger was just a couple steps behind. "It's not a loan, Scarlett. I'm *giving* the money to you."

"I'd rather stick with the loan."

"Scarlett!" Now he raised his voice, his stare like the scope of a sniper. "Why are you behaving this way?"

Now it was my turn to snap. "You're a *billionaire*. I've busted my ass for you the last five years, and you've paid me cents on the euro. Then I come to you to pursue something I've always been passionate about, and you *hesitate*?" Axel didn't hesitate. He wanted me to open the biggest restaurant I possibly could rather than play it safe with that hole-in-the-wall. "I felt like I'd walked into a bank and applied for a loan and the underwriter had to review all my finances first."

"I told you I just needed time to accept your decision—"

"Well, I need some time to accept your money." I left the chair and carried my dish to the counter. "You didn't even like the food…"

"I did like it—"

"Then why didn't you eat it?" I rounded on him, my back to the counter.

"I'd just eaten before I came over here."

"Axel could have just eaten an ox, and he still would have eaten all of it." I turned back to the counter and grabbed a glass container to store the leftovers in the hope I would try it later…when I actually had an appetite.

My father came to my side. "Sweetheart, let's just calm down—"

"You don't believe in me."

"That's not true."

"I wanted to open a restaurant before, but all you cared about was the business."

"Because that business was built with my bare hands." He tried to keep his voice low, but it started to rise with his anger.

"I didn't want to marry Axel, but you talked me into it. I wanted to open the restaurant, but you talked me out of it. You told me that I would be able to run the business after you're gone, but we've been ambushed twice, and you don't seem to understand why I want to step away. It seems like all you care about is yourself."

He stilled, his eyes flicking back and forth between mine. For once, he didn't have anything to say.

I couldn't believe I'd just said that to him. "I think you should go."

The anger in his eyes was quickly replaced by fear. "You know you're the single most important thing in the world to me. I'm sorry that I ever made you question that. I'm sorry that the business was pulled out from underneath us and forced me to make these hard decisions. I'm sorry that I made you feel like you don't matter. That I don't believe in your cooking or in your success as a chef and a business owner. I'm sorry for all of it."

I turned away, moved by his words but refusing to show it.

"Sweetheart—"

"I just need some space right now." I wouldn't look at him. I was so furious with him, and I wasn't sure why. Like a switch had been flipped and light flooded the room, I saw the world in a different way. I couldn't explain it. All I could do was feel it.

He remained next to me, lingering against the counter like he was trying to search for the right words to change my mind. But he seemed to realize that the more he pursued me, the more he would push me away. "Goodnight, sweetheart." He left the kitchen and entered the living room. The sound of his loafers tracked his location through the apartment. Then I heard the front door open and shut.

That was when I knew he was gone.

# Chapter 8

## *Axel*

Two weeks.

It'd been two weeks since I'd last seen her. Since I'd last heard from her.

Every day was just as agonizing as the one before, and I started to wonder if it would ever get better. A part of me hoped she would realize she couldn't live without me and come back.

But she didn't.

There were times when I wanted to text. Times when I wanted to stop by her apartment just to see how she was doing. But since she was the one who'd decided to leave the relationship, I wasn't in a position to do that. If I pursued her, it wouldn't be romantic, just harassment.

Times like these made me reconsider killing Dante. If I couldn't have her, then neither could he.

I was on the couch in my bedroom, my date for the evening a decanter of scotch, when Aldo knocked on the door.

I was still pissed at him for the fiasco with Theo, so I ignored him.

Aldo knocked again.

"Fuck off. I'm not hungry."

"Sir, Scarlett is here to see you."

In a nanosecond, my world changed. The dull grays suddenly turned brilliant. A rush of emotion burst through me and erased the numbness. I moved off the couch so quickly that I tripped and stumbled forward before catching myself on the other couch. I made my way to the door and ripped it open so hard it swung around and made a dent in the wall. "She's here. Now?"

"She's waiting in the parlor."

My heart raced so fast that it made me realize I hadn't had a heartbeat these last two weeks. Adrenaline. Endorphins. Ecstasy. Everything rushed through me like a needle had just been injected into my arm. "Did she say why she's here?"

"No."

"Does she have papers with her?" Divorce papers. I hadn't filed, and if she really wanted to be free of me, she would have to do the dirty work herself.

"Not that I recall, sir. But I suppose her purse is big enough to stash some paperwork..." He stared at me.

I stared back.

"Will you see her?"

"Yes, I just need a minute."

"Of course." He reached around and grabbed the door before he shut it.

I walked into the bathroom and quickly rinsed my mouth to hide the evidence of the scotch. I was in just my sweatpants without a shirt and I considered changing, but then I realized it was nearly eight o' clock and she knew I was never dressed when I was home. Didn't want to make it seem like I tried too hard. Until I knew the purpose of her visit, I didn't want her to see my hand. I wasn't the kind of guy to play games, but this was a match I had to win.

I headed downstairs and approached the parlor. The double doors were open, and Aldo had already prepared a fire. She sat in one of the armchairs, her gaze on the flames, the light blanketing her features in a tantalizing glow. It was the first time I'd seen her since she'd left, and I couldn't bring myself to look at her pictures on my phone because it would only make her absence hurt more. I was rooted to the spot, remembering the softness of her cheek when my fingers brushed against it. Our estrangement had been brief, but it felt like years since I'd seen her. She even looked different, like it'd been two years instead of two weeks.

I stepped into the room, and her head immediately turned when she heard me. Instead of remaining in her chair, she got to her feet, her hands immediately coming together at her waist, something she did when she was nervous.

I stared at her.

She stared at me.

My heart raced like an off-beat drum.

Her expression was composed, but her eyes were a little wider than they normally were, showing the same adrenaline that I was sure raced in her veins.

I came closer to her, standing near the fire.

She didn't look at my bare chest, her eyes glued to mine.

I glanced at her bag on the table. The top was closed, so I couldn't see the contents inside. My eyes flicked back to hers, desperate to know the reason for her visit. If she wanted me back, I expected a different reception than this guarded one. If she wanted a divorce, she could just mail the papers.

She broke eye contact first, her breaths so elevated that her chest visibly rose and fell. She looked at the fire for a few seconds before she found the strength to look at me again. But no words were forthcoming.

I didn't want to speak first. I wanted to know what she wanted before I made an idiot out of myself.

But she still didn't talk.

"If you have something to say, you should say it. Otherwise, I'm going to kiss you. I'm going to kiss you and make love to you. I'm going to make love to you and tie you up so you can't leave me again."

Her gaze flicked away, and the firelight reflected off the tears in her eyes. She took a deep breath to steady herself, and that told me that these last few weeks had been as agonizing for her as they'd been for me.

I hadn't taken off my wedding ring since the day I'd put it on. I still wore it now—because I hoped she would come back. Being married to the wrong person in the past had shown me I was married to the right person now. But there was a fucking snake in our bed, biting at our heels and making us bleed.

"I—I wanted to talk to you." She wasn't the confident woman that I knew. She was practically in shambles, so unsure of herself that she couldn't stand still. Her body swayed slightly like a flower stem in the breeze. She couldn't hold eye contact for long, always darting her gaze away when it became too much for her.

I swallowed the disappointment. "Say what you want to say."

She moved back to the armchair that she'd occupied previously.

My fantasy of a scorching-hot kiss in front of the blazing fireplace was extinguished. The disappointment was bitter, and the anger was sharp. It took me a second to move to the corner of the couch closest to her and give her my attention without looking enraged.

She stared at her hands for a moment. "I talked to my father..."

I sucked in a sharp breath, feeling an accumulation of shock and hope. I'd begged him to tell her the truth so I could get her back, but that request had seemed to fall on deaf ears. But perhaps seeing how miserable she was gave him a change of heart.

"He told me that love deserves a second chance sometimes."

My heart dropped like a stone in a flat pond. The ripples stretched out endlessly.

"He believes you really love me."

Anyone who saw us together would believe that. "You came here to talk about us, but it sounds like you only want to talk about your father." My temper made me lash out like an angry child. It was stupid on my part, but I was pissed off that Dante didn't do the right thing and tell her the truth. He took the coward's way out and tried to get around his lies.

She flinched at the aggression in my voice. "I'm trying to tell you I've thought things over—"

"No, your father whispered in your ear, and whatever opinion he has, you have."

Her eyes flicked back and forth between mine in horror.

She'd come here to work things out, but I was too pissed off to care. I chose to burn down the house—and our relationship with it. "I'm tired of being in bed with your father. I'm tired of this being a fucking threesome. I'm tired of your father having the power to interfere and influence this relationship with the snap of his fingers. Scarlett, we're married, which means we're family. But I've never been treated like family."

Her eyes continued to water. "I said I want to work on this relationship—"

"There is no working on this relationship," I snapped. "I've kissed the ground you walk on from the moment I saw you. Your father is the one who tore us apart like a flimsy piece of paper. You either believe me or you don't—and you clearly don't. I spoke to your father last week and fucking begged him to come clean, but he refused. Instead, he chose to stay in the shadows and pull your strings like the puppet you are. Tried to get the same outcome without the transparency. That's not how I want you, Scarlett. I want you to march in here and tell me you love me and can't live without me. You think sitting here listening to you say your father gave his approval of our relationship makes me hard? You think that's romantic? You think I want to hear that shit?" I got to my feet and moved back to the fire. "I haven't left the house in two weeks. I've been fucking miserable. Sitting around waiting for you to pull your head out of your ass and come back to me. But that's clearly not going to happen. So get the fuck out of my house."

She was still on the armchair, her eyes wet and reflecting the firelight.

"I'm obviously an idiot because I only fall for the wrong women. My first wife burned my life to the ground, but I think you're a bigger mistake because I should have known better by now." I lit the match and poured gasoline on the fire. Even though she was on the verge of sobs, I kept going. "I deserve better than this. I deserve better than *you*."

That last statement broke her, and the sheen in her eyes deepened into tears. Her bottom lip quivered as the sobs tried to break out of her chest. She reached for her purse, and with her head down, she rushed past me and out the door.

I let her go. I let her walk out of my life—for the last time.

---

Theo emptied his glass with a final sip before he returned it to the table. "You must feel better if you're out of the house."

We sat together in a quiet bar, most of the patrons gone for the night. The bar was supposed to be closed, but they kept it open for us. Nothing good happened at two a.m.—and truer words had never been spoken. "I saw my lawyer today. Filed for divorce."

Theo's eyes widened at the statement. His reactions were always muted and subtle, but this elicited a visceral response. "I thought you were going to talk to Dante."

"I did." I pulled my phone out of my pocket, opened the file, and then pressed play. Our voices sounded in the quiet bar, the two of us talking in his parlor as I implored him to grow a pair of balls and man up to his mistakes. The recording was about ten minutes long, and once Theo got the gist of the conversation, I stopped it.

Theo picked up his cigar and stared at me. "Is there a reason you haven't played that for Scarlett?"

"I shouldn't have to." I returned the phone to my pocket. Scarlett hadn't texted me since she'd left my home the other day, not that I expected her to. She could have been in my bed that night, her soft thighs around my hips, but I was done.

"It's her father—"

"If she opened her fucking eyes, she would know it's true just based on the other shit he does." He walked all over her like a damn doormat, and she tolerated it. "She came to my place the other night and said she wanted to work on things."

"Isn't that a good thing?"

"It's not when she prefaces it by telling me that her father encouraged her to do it."

Theo gave a slight nod in understanding. "He's trying to get around it."

"Coward."

"At least he feels guilty enough to try. Maybe he's not as much of a psychopath as I thought."

"He's not a psychopath," I said. "He's evil—that's what the fuck he is." I brought the cigar to my lips and let the smoke flood my mouth. It was licorice, my least favorite flavor.

"Maybe you should sleep on this—"

"I have slept on it. I'm done." I released the smoke from my mouth. "I've only loved two women—and they were both mistakes."

"I don't think it's fair to compare Scarlett to that bitch."

"She's a mistake, nonetheless."

"Scarlett didn't lie to take your money and get you thrown in jail. She didn't destroy your relationship with your parents. It's fine to be upset, but the comparison is not only inaccurate, but insulting to Scarlett."

"Didn't realize you liked Scarlett so much."

He shrugged. "She's a victim in an abusive relationship—and she doesn't even realize it. Simple as that." He brought the cigar to his mouth and sank back in his chair. "I agree that you've earned her trust, but people are complicated."

"It's not that complicated."

He pulled the cigar away and let the smoke release. "I can tell you've made up your mind, so I'll leave it be."

"Good," I said. "Because I haven't felt this good in weeks."

# Chapter 9

## *Scarlett*

I stopped cooking.

I stopped showering.

I stopped living.

I slept for three days on and off. Sometimes on the couch, sometimes on the rug in the living room, sometimes on the bed. In and out of consciousness, I drifted, my heart and soul so broken my mind shut down to protect everything else. The only time I ate was when a migraine knocked on my front door. Then I ate a small amount of whatever I could find in the kitchen, just enough to stop the pain before it could really start. I had the TV on the whole time just for background noise in the apartment, but I never really watched it. The voices of the actors made me feel less alone.

Axel never called or stopped by to apologize for what he'd said. It was the harshest thing he'd ever said to me, and when no apology came, I knew he'd meant it. His words weren't just spoken out of anger. They were spoken from the heart.

I was a mistake.

A regret.

That man always fought for me, and now I lived in a world where he didn't want me anymore. Even if I crawled back to him, he probably wouldn't even speak to me. He'd shut the door in my face and tell me to disappear.

Just a few weeks ago, we were happy. Talking about the two kids he wanted to have. And now I was just a mistake.

I got a few messages from vendors that wanted to partner with my restaurant, but those messages went unanswered. I had so much to do, but now I didn't have the heart to bother. Running a restaurant had once been my passion, but now I couldn't picture myself ever cooking again.

My father texted me a few times too, asked how I was doing, hoped I was having a good day, asked if he could see me.

I ignored them all.

There was no one in the world I wanted to see right now. No one I wanted to talk to. I'd rather stare at the wall in silence than try to carry on like nothing had happened, like Axel's final words wouldn't haunt me for the rest of my life.

I was on the couch when someone knocked on the door.

I immediately muted the TV and remained quiet, hoping the person would just walk away.

But they knocked again. "Sweetheart, I just want to check on you."

A rush of disappointment moved through me, and I hated myself for that.

"You gave me a spare key, remember?"

I still didn't move from the couch, calling his bluff.

But I heard the key move into the lock, and then the doorknob turned. He stepped inside, and his eyes immediately found mine, turning sad. "Sweetheart..." He must have seen the days of tears coated on my cheeks, must have seen the look of death in my eyes because he came to the couch and moved his arm around me.

My head automatically dipped to his shoulder, and I started to cry.

He squeezed me hard as his chin rested on my head. "Please don't cry, baby girl."

---

With a wad of wet tissues tucked in my closed hand, I sat next to him on the couch. "I went to his place and shared everything you said to me, that love deserved a second chance and how much Axel loved me...but that just made him angry."

"Why?"

"Because he thinks I only changed my mind because you changed it." I couldn't explain everything, not without breaking my promise to Axel. It was hard to sit there and keep it to myself, to not confront my father about the horrible allegations. But I kept my mouth shut because I still loved Axel, even if he didn't care for me anymore. "Said he's tired of being in a relationship with not just me, but you."

My father stared at the coffee table.

"Then he..." It was hard to replay this part of the conversation because it was so devastating. "Said that I was a bigger mistake than his first wife...and he deserves better than me." New tears sprung to my eyes, but I blinked them away. "Kicked me out of his house. Said he's done with me." It somehow hurt more to repeat it than to go through it in the first place. It was still raw, a flesh wound so new it hadn't even had the chance to stop bleeding.

My father was quiet for a long time, clearly at a loss for what to say.

I suddenly felt cold and pulled the blanket over myself. Sleeping all the time and not eating made my body function differently. I didn't have the energy to keep my body warm, and with every passing day, I seemed to grow colder.

"Give him space. I'm sure he spoke out of anger."

"He did speak out of anger, but he meant every word he said."

He rubbed his palm across the stubble of his jawline and gave a sigh. "I'll talk to him."

"I'd rather you not. Just leave it alone."

"I don't appreciate the way he spoke to you—"

"Please." I turned to him, my wet eyes pleading. "Just leave it alone."

He stared into my eyes, the sadness heavy in his gaze. It was like looking in a mirror because my sadness reflected perfectly across his features. His eyes were depthless in their sorrow. His shoulders even sagged, which was noticeable in a man who always maintained a rigid posture. His skin was even a little pale, like the blood had left his extremities and flooded his organs. "I hate seeing you like this."

"I know you do. I'm sorry."

"No," he said with a deep breath. "I'm the one who's sorry."

"It's not your fault."

He looked away, staring at the shelves mounted on the wall, his eyes glazing over. "But it is."

# Chapter 10

## *Axel*

I walked into the restaurant and found Theo sitting alone at a table. It was his place because he preferred to pay himself rather than pay someone else. I moved between the tables and sat in the chair across from him. A glass of scotch was already waiting for me.

I picked it up and took a drink. "Better than pussy."

Theo gave a shrug. "Depends on the pussy."

"I've never had any that compares to this."

"Really?" he asked, cocking his head slightly.

I took another drink. "Nope."

"Seem to be in good spirits."

"Why wouldn't I be?"

"I figured the rage would have worn off by now."

I grabbed the menu and took a look. "What's the news on the Colombians?"

Theo took a drink. "Want to meet us on Tuesday."

"Good." Business had halted, and the ramifications were painful. Our profits were squeezed because we ate the costs so we wouldn't have to drop our workers. If we did, the whole system would collapse. I turned the menu over and continued to look.

Theo glanced down before he looked at me again.

"What?"

"You're still wearing your wedding ring."

I glanced at my left hand, the black band sitting exactly where I'd worn it since the day I got married. "I forgot it was there."

"Right."

"When you get used to wearing something, you forget about it—"

"Sure."

I gave him a cold stare before I looked at the menu again.

"The anger has an expiration date, but the pain doesn't."

"What the fuck do you want from me, Theo?" I dropped the menu.

He gave a shrug before he took a drink again.

I sat back in the chair, annoyed that I'd come out with Theo.

"It's not too late to fix things with Scarlett."

"I don't want to fix things with her."

"I think you know you lost your temper and fucked everything up, and it's easier to be angry than to admit you would be between her legs right now if you just let it go."

"Are you my therapist now?" I snapped. "I told you I'm over it."

"Then how many women have you slept with?"

I looked away. "You know I've never talked about that—"

"So, none."

"Like I would tell you—"

"None." He held up his hand and made a circle with his fingers. "Zero."

"Is this why you invited me to dinner?" I asked incredulously. "To grill me about this?"

"Why else?" he asked. "You think I enjoy your company?"

I took a drink. "I certainly don't enjoy yours."

He sank in his chair and said nothing else, the interrogation finally over.

My eyes drifted across the restaurant, seeing couples and friends having a meal together. Quiet conversation and occasional laughter filled the room. We were at the end of winter and the beginning of spring, but it still felt like the dark ages.

Theo rose from his chair. "Excuse me." He didn't push in his chair before he walked away.

I actually enjoyed his absence, enjoyed having a moment to digest the rage he'd just instilled in me. My elbow was propped on the armrest with my closed fist under my chin. My thumb started to turn the wedding ring on my finger, feeling the cool metal against my skin. It was a habit I'd picked up in my quiet moments, when I was deep in concentration.

Someone appeared in my peripheral and then came directly into my line of sight.

In his black blazer and collared shirt, Dante pulled out the chair and helped himself to the table, sitting directly across from me like we were a pair of friends who met up for dinner. His eyes were on the table for a moment, like he didn't want to look at me, like it physically caused him pain. After a breath, he overcame his rage and met my stare.

I stopped fidgeting with my ring.

He stared.

I stared.

I knew it was a setup. Dante must have conspired with Theo to get an audience with me, and there was only one reason he'd want to do that. Rage bubbled underneath my skin, but I suppressed it behind my scowl.

He didn't speak, like stringing together a couple words was too hard for him.

I let the silence linger, wanting to make it as hostile as possible.

"I gave you what you wanted." He didn't have the same eyes as Scarlett, but there were other parts of her that I saw in his face. Her expression was similar when she was angry, when she was guarded. "You asked for my daughter, and I gave her to you."

It was one of those rare situations where I was so angry, I expressed that rage as a laugh. A quiet, low laugh. "I don't want a puppet. I want a woman. I want a woman who chooses me, who chooses me despite her father's protests, not because of his approval. I've given that woman all of me, and I'm tired of it. So, you win, Dante. Congratulations. You've successfully destroyed the best thing that ever happened to your daughter." I straightened in my chair and brought my palms together, clapping loudly and slowly, catching the attention of the entire restaurant until the room turned silent. I sank back into my chair and stopped, and gradually, the conversations resumed.

Dante rested both elbows on the armrests with his hands together, staring at me as he tried to figure out his next play. "It hurts to see my daughter heartbroken like this—"

"You said she was relieved it was over." I cocked my head to the side. "Did you not?"

He remained quiet.

"Unless you're a liar? A coward and a liar?"

He started to rub his knuckles. "I didn't realize how she felt about you."

"I told you she loved me."

"You said you *thought* she loved you."

"No, I *knew*," I snapped. "I told you that, and you chose to disregard it."

He sucked in the hollows of his cheeks before he continued. "This is not easy for me—"

"Good."

He ignored me and continued. "But seeing my daughter cry all day...was one of the shittiest things I've ever been through. I know you love my daughter. Please give her another chance—"

"No."

"You said you wanted my daughter. You *have* her."

"But it's only a part of her. A very small part. The rest of her is locked inside a golden cage that I can't reach. She's always got one foot in the room and the other in the hall. She never fully lives in the moment with me because she's thinking about how I dumped her for some woman who doesn't hold a candle to her. And you know what? A part of me doesn't blame her. She shouldn't be with a man who would do that. She's too good for that. Our relationship is irrevocably destroyed—because of you."

"It's not irrevocably destroyed—"

"It's over, Dante."

"It's not over if you keep wearing your ring."

My hand had been underneath the table the entire time, so there was no way he could have seen it. That meant Theo had told him previously.

"Please talk to her. I've given her to you as you asked—"

"I want to clear my name. I want her to know that I've been loyal and committed to her since the moment she was mine. I want her to know the truth, Dante. That's what I fucking want. Convincing her to forgive my cheating ass is not what I asked."

His eyes darted away, his hands continuing to massage his knuckles. He seemed to fade from the conversation because he didn't look at me. He remained distant, like the request was ridiculous. But then he looked at me again. "If I tell her, will you work it out with her?"

The room was suddenly silent because the conversations were blocked out by the sound of my racing heart. I felt so much adrenaline, enough to fuel me for a fistfight with twelve opponents. My true desire had been dropped right in front of my face, within arm's reach. But it was bitter-sweet. Because I'd already told her the truth and she didn't believe me—and we'd never overcome that. The truth was staring her right in the face, but she couldn't see it. Instead, she believed the lies. We'd been married for months, and she continued to hold on to the past instead of stepping into the future with me. "No."

His eyes narrowed at the revelation.

I was just as surprised by my answer. "But if you love your daughter, you'll tell her the truth—because she deserves to know."

# Chapter 11

## *Scarlett*

I sat in the armchair in the living room, a warm cup of coffee on the end table beside me. It was afternoon, the sunlight coming through the open curtains and flooding the room with the first warmth I'd felt since the beginning of fall. I wasn't sure how long I sat there. Didn't bother to take a sip of my coffee.

I somehow felt worse now than I had when I'd watched Axel walk into that restaurant with Cassandra.

Didn't think that was possible.

I left him, so a clean break was what I should want, but I felt like I'd made the biggest mistake of my life. The man of my dreams had been at my fingertips, but now he was out of reach. The loss was so inconsolable I wasn't sure why I'd left in the first place. I felt guilty, like I'd made the wrong decision, like I was in the wrong.

A knock sounded on my door.

My eyes immediately flicked to the door and stared at the wood, taking a moment to realize that someone wanted to speak to me. It wasn't Axel. He hadn't come to my doorstep to apologize for his ruthless words. If he were going to ask for my forgiveness, he wouldn't have waited so long.

I left the armchair and slowly walked to the front door, taking so long that whoever was there had probably already moved on. Without checking the peephole, I opened it, indifferent to whoever was on the other side.

It was a man I didn't know.

Wordlessly, he held up the heavy envelope that must be stuffed with a hundred papers. "You've been served." He held it out for me to take.

I stared at the manila envelope, knowing the contents without opening the flap.

When I didn't take it, he tossed it at my feet. "Have a good day."

---

I cried for the rest of the day. Cried to the point that I gave myself a migraine and had to pop a couple pills and force myself to sleep it off. When I woke up, it was dark, and a glance at the clock on the nightstand told me it was almost eight in the evening.

I'd slept a long time—but not enough.

The packet of papers was still in the living room, unopened. I didn't know what a divorce looked like, but I knew it would be ugly. He hadn't asked me to sign any prenuptial agreements before our wedding day, so I was entitled to half his assets. But I would forfeit everything.

Because I only wanted him—not his money.

I collected my things and got in the car, driving to the only sanctuary left to me. I pulled through the gates, ignored the guards with heavy guns on the property, and then walked through the front doors.

The sound of voices was immediately audible, along with the uproarious laughter of two men.

My father must have company.

His butler appeared from the other room, slightly flustered because he clearly hadn't expected another guest. "Good evening, Scarlett. Is your father expecting you?"

"No." I'd come all the way here to find comfort in his arms, but he had other arrangements. "I should have called first. Let me him know I stopped by." I started to turn away.

"Your father has never hesitated to drop whatever he's doing for you, so let me speak with him." He moved in front of the doorway to cut me off, something he'd never done before. He was always distant and withdrawn, knowing his place as the help. "Please stay here. I'll be right back." He eyed me hesitantly, like he could see the devastation all over my face. I always wore makeup, but I hadn't worn it in weeks. My clothes were wrinkled too, because I didn't bother to hang them up anymore. Just tossed them on the floor to be retrieved at a later time.

Once he realized I wouldn't walk off, he left the room to speak to my father.

It took less than two minutes for my father to rush into the room, his footsteps quick like he was on the brink of a sprint. His eyes found mine, and a blanket of sadness covered his face. He moved to me, empathy bright in his eyes like Christmas lights. "Sweetheart, what's happened?"

"I didn't know you had company."

"Doesn't matter if I have company. You're all that matters." He gripped me by the arm then pulled me into him, securing his arms around me in a warm hug. His chin went to the top of my head. "Tell me what's wrong."

I held my silence, letting his warmth dull the pain until it wore off. "Axel served me divorce papers today." I stepped away and presented the packet of papers from my purse before I set it down.

My father hesitated before he took them. He bent the metal prongs straight to open the flap, and then he pulled out the papers so he could read the first few sentences. His eyes shifted back and forth as he read, and then he gave a sigh when he'd read enough. "Goddammit." He shoved the papers back inside before he tossed the envelope on the table. He took a few steps away, his fingers dragging across his jawline in annoyance. He gave another frustrated sigh.

"I didn't expect this to happen so quickly." I'd expected Axel to apologize for the way he'd ripped into me and left me to bleed. He had such a good heart and an award-winning smile. He simply wasn't the kind of man that was even capable of such savagery. I'd hoped he'd just spoken out of anger, but he clearly hadn't...or he was still that angry.

"Nor did I." He sat on the couch, his elbows on his knees.

I sat across from him, unsure what I expected my father to do. He'd always fixed my problems, always knew what to do in any situation. His counsel and advice had always been gold to me. But I knew this was something he couldn't fix. "Maybe you could talk to him." It was futile, but this was not how I wanted our marriage to end. I didn't want to be another regret. I didn't want to be compared to *her*.

My father lifted his chin and looked at me. "I already have."

What little hope I had left slowly tumbled down into the pit of my stomach. I swallowed and gave a nod.

His chin dipped again. "Sweetheart, I'm so sorry."

"It's okay," I whispered. "It's not your fault."

His chin remained down, eyes on the rug.

I stared at him, watching his features closely, my heart racing a little quicker with every passing second. Heat flushed into my cheeks, my emotions running hot as if they were bottled inside my chest. *It's not your fault...right?* The question repeated inside my head several times, but I couldn't ask it. Despite the doubts, despite the desperation, I couldn't break my promise to Axel. All I could do was pierce my father's flesh with my stare, examine his features for information his words couldn't provide.

He remained that way, eyes down for minutes, his hands clasped.

I inhaled a slow breath then shifted my gaze away, feeling guilty for questioning my father, the one person who loved me unconditionally. But then I felt just as shitty for questioning Axel, who loved me with all his heart. "You should go back to your dinner. I wouldn't have come if I'd known."

After a heavy sigh, he lifted his chin. "In any other circumstance, I would send my guest away and take you out for gelato or something. But it's an important client. Made a long trip to speak with me."

I felt a flash of disappointment, but I knew that was selfish. "Those divorce papers aren't going anywhere. We can talk tomorrow."

"Thank you for understanding." He rose to his feet then kissed me on the forehead. "It's going to be alright, sweetheart."

I nodded against his chest even though I didn't believe him.

He kissed me again before he let me go. "Gelato tomorrow?"

I nodded.

He gave me a smile, but it was the forced kind that didn't reach his eyes. "I look forward to it." He released me and returned to the hallway and then the dining room. "My apologies. How's the wine?"

"I prefer French wine, but it's not bad." He spoke with a French accent.

I walked out the door and got into the car. I didn't start the engine, and I just sat there in the dark driveway, looking out the dirty windshield. Now that I didn't park my car on the street, it stayed cleaner longer, but the rain had stained it with waterdrops.

It was stupid to think my father would erase my pain the way he erased all my other problems. But he'd always been my hero, the man I looked up to, and knowing that he spoke to Axel but the outcome hadn't changed devastated me. Our relationship couldn't be salvaged. Whether Axel was lying or telling the truth, it seemed like this relationship had always been doomed to fail, from the first moment we'd met and he'd pursued me while I already had a man in my life.

It was never meant to be.

I didn't know how long I sat there in the dark, but I didn't think about driving away until it started to get cold. I hit the button to start the engine, but the dashboard didn't light up. The car remained quiet. I hit the button again, and nothing happened. "What the...?" I tried a couple more times but then realized the problem. "My purse..." I'd left it on the coffee table when I'd pulled out the divorce papers.

It took all my strength to get out of the car and walk back when all I wanted to do was collapse on the couch again.

But I pushed the car door open, crossed the pavers and stepped up to the door once again. I let myself into the house and walked across the room to where my purse sat, the envelope of papers sitting beside it.

"This is what we'll do," I heard my father say. "I spoke to the Colombians privately and offered them a higher fee than they even asked for if they'd choose to align themselves with this new partnership. The distribution channels that Theo set up are already in place, so I don't need him anymore. You take out Axel and Theo, and once they're gone, we'll split the business fifty-fifty."

I had just reached for my purse, but I halted when I heard what my father said.

My blood ran cold.

I stilled like a statue, as if my father would know I was there if I breathed too loudly, even though there was a wall between us.

My heart was like a drum in a marching band, pounding harder as I had more time to absorb the horrible thing he'd just said. He said it so simply, like he had no hesitation or doubt, like taking a life was child's play.

I knew the butler would realize I was there because the door had opened and shut, so I couldn't linger. I wanted to listen and see what else he had to say, but I couldn't get caught. I grabbed my purse and the papers and quickly walked out of the house, careful to close the door behind me as gently as possible.

I hopped into the car and took off without fastening my safety belt.

I just had to get out of there.

———

Instead of going home, I headed to Axel's.

I checked in with Aldo in the entryway. "I need to speak with him. Is he home?" It was almost ten now, so he was either home on the couch in his bedroom or...he was out. Doing god knows what.

"Wait in the parlor, and I'll let him know you're here."

"Thanks, Aldo."

He headed to the stairs then disappeared on to the next floor.

I walked into the parlor. I'd left my purse in the car along with the mountain-sized stack of paperwork Axel had served me. Instead of taking a seat, I stood in front of the cold fireplace, remembering the last conversation we'd had in this room. It had echoed in my mind every day since I'd run for cover.

Aldo returned minutes later—alone. "He says he doesn't want to see you." He stood with his arms behind his back, his look somber, like he truly regretted what he had to say. "I'm sorry, Scarlett."

I blinked a couple times as I processed the rejection. Axel had always been there for me, at my beck and call, and now I knew how it felt to be like everyone else. To be unremarkable. Unimportant. It fucking hurt. "I—I really need to speak with him."

"There's nothing I can do," he said quietly. "He's been in a mood since you were last here."

So he was still pissed off. Really pissed off. I looked out the double doors into the hallway and swallowed. "I need to see him, and I'm not leaving here until I do." I moved through the double doors and toward the stairs.

"Scarlett." Aldo's frantic voice came from behind me. "I can't let you do that."

"Then you're going to have to manhandle me," I said as I took two steps at a time. "And good luck with that."

"Scarlett." He continued to chase me, going around the banister and up the next flight of stairs behind me. "I promise you this is not a good idea. Stop. I said, stop."

I made it to the hallway and walked at a brisk pace, my pulse pounding in my neck and making the skin throb. The door was in sight, and the adrenaline made me glide across the runner over the wooden floorboards.

"Scarlett, don't go in there."

I stopped at the door and looked at him, the horror hitting me in the chest. "Why? Does he... Is there someone in there?"

He heaved as he caught up to me, bent slightly at the waist because the stairs took a toll on him. It took him seconds to form words, like he hadn't gotten that much exercise in decades, even though he walked up those stairs every single day.

"Does he?" I repeated, afraid of the answer.

His hands went to his hips, and he stopped in front of me. "Yes."

A sledgehammer hit me right in the chest, breaking all my ribs and then smashing my heart. I didn't know I could be so heartbroken and so nauseous at the same time, but I was about to vomit on the rug.

Aldo lowered his voice. "Come on, let's go."

Just as I took a step away, the door opened.

There Axel stood, in nothing but his sweatpants, both beautiful and terrifying. His blue eyes were cold like the Arctic Circle, and that harsh stare seemed to be permanently reserved for me. He regarded me as his enemy, not his friend, not his wife. It was like he hated me. "What do you want?"

All I could picture was another blonde in his bed, a woman without a face but with huge tits and a juicy ass, sleeping in the bed that had belonged to me just two weeks ago. "If you're already fucking around, I guess I never meant that much to you." My time alone had been spent with wine and tears. His had been spent with scotch and tits. I didn't bother sharing what I'd come all the way down here to tell him. It seemed significant knowing he had already kissed someone else, fucked someone else...

His eyes narrowed. "What did you just say to me?"

I sidestepped Aldo and headed down the hallway.

He raised his voice. "I asked you a question."

I ignored him, barely able to contain my tears at this point.

Aldo spoke with a trembling voice. "I didn't know how else to stop her, so I told her you were with someone—"

"*You did what?*"

I stopped when I got to the stairs, stilled by the rage in his voice.

"You're dismissed, Aldo. Pack up your shit and leave. Now."

I peeked over my shoulder, seeing the two men stare each other down.

"I'm sorry, sir," Aldo said. "You said you didn't want to see her and—"

"Leave my sight." Axel's eyes shifted to me. "And *you*." His eyes narrowed on me, vicious and scathing. "You came all the way down here to say something, so say it. Get your ass back over here and tell me what's so goddamn important that you would defy my wishes and get my butler canned."

Aldo bowed his head and walked to the staircase, his eyes purposely down to avoid my stare. He passed me and took the stairs, his footsteps disappearing after a few seconds.

Now it was just me and Axel—and I was terrified.

Axel continued to stare me down with ferocity. "I said, get your ass over here."

I turned back to the stairs. "I don't want to meet my replacement—"

"Get your ass over here, or I'll make you."

I gripped the banister and breathed hard, all the little hairs on my arms standing on edge. "Don't tell me what to do—"

"Don't barge into my house like you own the place. You're the one who took your shit and left." He raised his voice.

"Now, get over here, or I swear to fucking Satan, I will throw you over my shoulder and toss you on the bed."

I started down the stairs.

"The hard way, then." He ran down the hallway, and the glimpse of him charging me reminded me of a bear chasing down its prey.

I rushed down the stairs.

He caught up to me effortlessly, and even at a downward angle, he grabbed me and hoisted me over his shoulder. It happened so fast, my face dropping to where my ass had been seconds ago, and the whole world flipped, the stairs above my head. My face was close to his ass, which was tight as hell in those sweatpants. "Jesus..."

He carried me up the stairs like I weighed nothing and into his bedroom. He flopped me down on the unmade bed.

When I hit the mattress, I bounced a little, and my body immediately remembered what it was like to sleep on this mattress, to feel us bounce together when he was on top of me.

His hands landed on either side of me, pinning me against the bed. "Does it look like anyone's here?" His eyes were sharp like broken glass, wanting to stab me all the way through. He pushed off me then stepped away, the muscles in his back muscular and tight. He paced for a moment, breathing through his rage, like just being in the same room with me was too much.

I sat up and moved to the edge of the bed before I got to my feet. With a quick scan, it seemed like Axel was telling the truth. There was no one else here but him. Aldo had fed me a lie to get rid of me, but he accidentally got rid of himself.

Axel turned to face me, his big arms crossed over his chest. His head was cocked slightly to the side, and he stared me down with impatience. "Is this about the divorce papers? All you have to do is sign them and drop them in the post. I enclosed my lawyer's information so he can handle it."

"It's not about that—"

"Then what the fuck do you want?" He took a step closer to me.

"If you would stop yelling at me and cutting me off every two seconds, then maybe I could get a sentence out," I snapped. "Jesus Christ."

He clenched his jaw. "I said I didn't want to see you."

"Well, we need to talk—"

"*We* don't need to do anything. There is no *we*. There hasn't been a *we* since you left me, since you packed up your stuff and walked out of my life. I used to be wrapped around your goddamn finger and would do anything for you, but that shit is over. Get used to it because I'm not your man anymore—"

"I believe you."

"Good," he barked. "Glad we're finally on the same page."

"I mean...I believe you about my father."

The tightness in his neck and arms suddenly went slack. All the rage that filled the air around us suddenly evaporated like water boiling in a pot. Even his breathing changed, going from short and shallow to slow and steady. His eyes narrowed then they widened again, as if he was replaying the conversation in his head because he was in disbelief.

"You were telling the truth." Distant tears started in my throat, hot and fresh, a dull burn. My sinuses started to hurt from the strain because ocean-sized tears were being restrained by that dam. "And I didn't believe you." I hadn't really had a chance to reflect on what had just happened with my father, to absorb his betrayal for the unforgivable backstab that it was. I hadn't even had a chance to accept it. I had no actual proof, but the words I'd overhead told me the truth about his character. "I'm so sorry..."

He inhaled a slow breath, and finally, the Axel I remembered came back to me. His eyes were still focused with powerful intensity, but it wasn't fused with anger anymore. It was simply intense, like the way he used to look at me. "And why do you believe me now?"

"Ever since I've been back at my apartment...I've had doubts."

"Doubts about what?"

"My father." My eyes flicked down, feeling guilty for thinking it and saying it. "Just things that he's said, things he's done. I got upset and asked him to leave. We didn't speak for several days."

"What were you upset about?"

"It's a long story—"

"You have my undivided attention." His eyes continued to bore into mine, aggressive but not irrational.

"I asked for a loan for my restaurant...and he said he had to think about it." My eyes shifted away. "Suggested that I think about returning to the family business, even though I made it very clear I'll never change my mind about that. It seemed like he didn't care about my wants and dreams— only his."

He listened to every word, not even blinking.

"So I got my own loan at the bank—"

"Attagirl."

I stilled at the affection in his voice, realizing just how much I'd missed it. "He came over, barely ate my cooking, and I just...got upset. Asked him to leave. We didn't talk for a while. I was angry with him, but I didn't really understand why. Now I do. It's because I had doubts... You were right."

His body stayed rigid, muscular arms over his hard chest.

"I've been miserable without you."

His stare remained hard, but there was a flicker of weakness, a blink of his eyes. But it was the first break in his rough exterior.

"You have no idea just how miserable."

"I have a pretty good idea."

I looked away, ashamed of my stupidity. "I wish I could take it back."

"Don't we all?"

My heart dropped into my stomach because I'd hoped I would be welcomed with open arms, that telling him this would change our circumstances, but he still seemed so angry. "I was just at my father's house to show him the papers you sent me, but he had someone over for dinner. I left and sat in the car for a while, so miserable that I just stared at the darkness. But then I realized I'd forgotten my purse, so I went back inside and heard my father say something...say something horrible."

His eyes narrowed. "And what did he say?"

"He asked someone to kill you and Theo."

Lashing out in anger would be an appropriate reaction, but he smirked instead, a slight smirk mixed with a frown. "He never learns, does he?"

"Maybe I misunderstood him—"

"Trust me, you didn't," he said. "Who was he speaking to?"

"I don't know. I didn't see him."

"Is there any identifying information you can provide me?"

At the time, all I'd cared about was what my father said, not who he'd said it to. "I think he was French."

"Why do you say that?"

"He said he preferred French wine, and he had a French accent."

Axel's eyebrows furrowed. "You didn't get a name? You didn't recognize his voice?"

I shook my head. "I'm sorry."

His left hand moved to his chin to rub the scruff on his jawline. He was so focused on the information I'd just shared that he didn't notice my stare.

He still wore his wedding ring.

*He still wore it.*

He paced for a moment, rubbing his bottom lip with his fingertips, his eyes glazed over in a haze. "Thank you for sharing this with me." He came back to me, both arms crossed over his chest again.

I'd expected more. I'd expected an embrace...a kiss...something.

But he continued to stand far away from me, treating me like a stranger.

"I miss you." I felt the tears form behind my eyes. He used to be all over me all the time, and now I realized how special that was. He'd made me feel loved long before he'd said it. He made every other guy in my life feel like a damn joke.

His eyes hardened at my admission, locking me out and throwing away the key.

"I love you—"

"You don't get to do that."

My body gave an involuntary flinch at his savagery. He had been barbaric to me during our last conversation, but I'd let it go because I knew he was more than his coldness in that moment. But it looked like that coldness was here to stay.

"You only believe me because you caught him red-handed."

"I didn't catch him red-handed. I heard him say something unrelated—"

"That he's conspiring to kill the man you love. Smoking gun."

My eyes flicked back and forth between his, hating the abrupt change in our relationship, the rift that couldn't be healed. "I'm sorry that I didn't believe you, but you must understand how complicated of a situation that was for me—"

"It's not complicated."

"He's all I've ever had. Do you have any idea how this will destroy me?" The tears broke free. "That the man I thought I could trust, no matter what, destroyed my marriage and hurt the man I love most? I haven't even had time to process this because I rushed straight here after I found out, because I care more about you right now."

His gaze was still hard as steel, showing he felt absolutely nothing.

"Please...give me another chance."

He looked away, staring at the wall for a few seconds before shifting his stare to the floor. "Your father gave me a choice. You or my parents. I chose my parents, but I somehow lost both of you. That man has single-handedly ruined my life, and I had to tolerate that destruction alone. I jumped through endless hoops to earn you, but when I finally trusted you enough to tell you the truth, you left me."

"What did you expect me to do? He's my father. You just said you picked your own father over me—"

"It would have been one thing if you just didn't believe me. But the fact that you left..." He shook his head. "The fact that you abandoned us when I've never once abandoned you...tells me everything I need to know."

The tears continued to drip down my cheeks. "You should have told me sooner—"

"What difference would it have made?" Now he started to yell again. "It would have made no difference—at all. Because you're blinded by your stupidity. If your father told you to jump off a bridge, you would. You're a fucking puppet with an invisible string. I looked your father in the eye and told him I loved you—and he still ripped us apart. He shot my father in the arm. You'll never understand how it feels to know that your parents despise you. I begged him to come clean with you and even told him I would help repair your broken relationship, and he still said no. And the fact that he still hasn't told you, even now..." He shook his head. "Shows me how little he respects you. How little he cares for you. You've known from the beginning that you were my whole world, and you threw it away."

I sobbed. It was all I could do.

"I'm done," he said simply. "We're buried in too much shit now."

"We love each other—"

"Loved."

"Loved?" I forced myself to stop crying. "I see your wedding ring..."

The hostility was instantaneous.

"I'm so sorry for everything. I mean that. I feel so terrible about everything you went through. But we're here, the facts are on the table, and it would be a waste not to finally have the relationship that was taken from us."

The storm clouds remained behind his eyes. "No."

"Axel—"

"I won't change my mind."

"You just said you begged my father to tell me the truth. That couldn't have been that long ago."

He said nothing.

"I'm sorry that I left. But I've been fucking miserable—"

"You've said this already," he said simply. "I'm not in the mood to hear it three or four times."

His perpetual coldness had finally iced my heart. This was not the man I'd fallen for. This was someone entirely new. His demeanor made me withdraw, made me pull back several feet even though my feet didn't take a step. "I'm sorry I didn't believe you, but you have to be the most heartless man on the planet not to understand how hard that would be. Even after hearing what my father said, it's still hard to believe he would do such a terrible thing, though I know it's true. My entire world has been shattered. I was fed lies by the person I trusted most, and the cost was the love of my life. I'm the victim in this as much as you are. Have some empathy and try to remember that."

Based on the way his eyes burned, he felt no empathy at all.

There was nothing I could say to bring Axel back. He was stubborn and angry, and my tears didn't soften that resolve at all. A continued conversation would just pull out the worst parts of him, the parts I didn't want to see. "I'll sign the papers and drop them in the mail."

"Good."

It felt like he'd shoved me into a pit of snakes. He didn't care how much he hurt me. He wanted to hurt me, wanted to cause me as much pain as he suffered. I would never see that boyish grin again. Never feel him pull me close and brush a kiss against my hairline. His laughter, the way he teased me, the brightness he brought into the world...they were all gone.

I only had one more thing to say before I left. "I'm sorry."

# Chapter 12

## *Axel*

I headed downstairs and found Aldo in his bedroom. There were two suitcases, meticulously organized to hold all of his things. The rest of his clothing was on hangers across the bed. His entire life had been reduced to his meager belongings. "Aldo."

He stilled when he heard my voice and turned around in a rush, his eyes guarded like he expected me to scream at him. "I'm almost done, sir. I'll be out of your hair in a second—"

"Why did you lie to her?"

He blinked several times, trying to come up with the right thing to explain his heinous actions. "I had no other way to stop her. I knew you would be angrier if I tried to grab her or restrain her."

"So you said I was sleeping around?"

"Actually, she assumed you had a woman in your bedroom, and I confirmed that belief so she would leave. I like Scarlett very much, but I knew it wouldn't be in her best interest to see you tonight when you've been so...upset."

Angry. The word was angry. "Unpack your things, Aldo."

"You—you aren't dismissing me?"

"Not tonight," I said. "But if you ever do that again, your ass will be on the street."

———

Theo joined me in the parlor, taking a seat in the armchair and firing up a cigar. He was always more interested in booze and smokes than he was in me. "I didn't expect to hear from you for a while."

"Trust me, your company is a great displeasure."

He smirked, like this was all a fucking game. "Still mad at me about that Dante thing?"

I gave him a scowl, feeling burning hatred for a man I once trusted. "What gave me away?"

"You know I had your best interests at heart."

"You deceived me."

"But it was for your own good."

"And what good did it do me?" I snapped.

He took his time pulling smoke into his mouth and releasing it from between his lips. "I don't like this new Axel. He's bitter like an old man who looks back on his life with regret. Even when you got out of prison, you weren't this bitter."

"Don't ever pull that shit again."

"Scarlett wants you. Isn't that what you've always wanted?"

"Under very different circumstances."

"We don't get to choose circumstances, asshole. We take what we get, roll with the punches. You know this."

I slouched in the chair. "I don't want to talk about her."

"Then why am I here?"

"Because I have more important shit to say." I stabbed the cigar into the ashtray, even though I'd just lit it a few minutes ago. "Dante is about to cross us."

He let the cigar rest between his fingertips, the smoke rising to the ceiling. There was little change to his expression, but it was clear he'd turned angry. "Is that so?"

"Scarlett overheard him talking to some French guy. He's already promised the Colombians a higher fee to work with him instead of us. And then this French asshole is supposed to take us out. They partner together and use all the arrangements you've already settled."

"And he thinks the Skull Kings would just allow this?" he asked incredulously.

"That's all the information Scarlett gave me. She left shortly afterward so she wouldn't be caught."

His eyes shifted away as he brought the cigar to his lips, pulling in the smoke as his mind became heavy with his thoughts. His eyes went still, and he considered this treason in silence. "What was Scarlett's reaction to this?" His eyes flicked back to mine.

"She finally believes me."

"Then you got what you wanted in the end."

I looked at the fire again. "Not really."

He gave a quiet sigh. "What the fuck is wrong with you?"

"She left me."

"It's not like she fucked another dick." He shook his head. "You love this woman, so why are you acting like a fucking lunatic—"

"Because I'm pissed off. That man ruined my life, and she took his side over mine."

"She didn't take sides—"

"She left, didn't she?" I snapped. "I gave her an ultimatum —she made her decision. She has to live with it now."

Theo studied me across the coffee table, judgment in his eyes. "Axel, let it go."

"No."

"I get you're pissed off, but this stubbornness will lead you down a dangerous road."

I shook my head. "I'm done." I crossed my arms over my chest and rested my ankle on the opposite knee. "I'm tired of bending over backward for that woman. I'm tired of busting my ass to be with her when she's never busted her ass for me. She has the divorce papers. All she has to do is sign them, and it's done."

Theo went quiet, and he was quiet for so long it seemed like he had nothing more to say.

I'd finally taken off my wedding ring. It was stashed in my nightstand drawer. I was tired of people staring at it and assuming it meant something when it meant nothing at all. I continued to look at my brother and waited for him to say something, to tell me I was an idiot, that I was making the biggest mistake of my life.

"So, you're certain?" Acceptance was in his voice.

"Yes." The conversation finally came to an end. I'd no longer have to defend myself.

"Then you wouldn't have a problem if I asked her out."

I felt all the muscles in my body stiffen simultaneously. A rock dropped into my stomach, and a cloud of dread suddenly blocked the sun. With narrowed eyes and a guarded stare, I regarded Theo with a subdued rage. "What the fuck did you just say?"

"You just said you were certain—"

"So your first instinct is to ask her out?"

"We both know she won't be single for long."

"Asshole, I know what you're doing. You're so full of it."

He took another puff of the cigar, let it absorb onto the surface of his tongue for the taste, and then released it. "What am I doing?"

"Trying to piss me off so I go back to her. It's not going to work."

He gave a slight shrug. "So, are you cool with it or not?"

I'd known Theo for a long time, and he was never one to bluff or bullshit. He seemed genuine as he sat across from me, and that started to make me uncomfortable. "Cut the shit."

"I'm being serious, Axel. I would never infringe on your territory without your permission, but if you really despise this woman so much, then I don't see why you would care—"

"I never said I despise her."

"Whatever. Yes or no?"

"She's my wife."

"And about to be your ex-wife because you sent her divorce papers."

"Why would you even want to see her—"

"Because she's sexy. I never told you this because you lose your shit every time it comes up, but the chemistry was there. There was fire, and it *burned*. I kept my distance because she was your woman, but she made it very clear she wanted to fuck my brains out, no strings attached, and use me like a fuckboy. So, if she really means nothing to you—"

"I never said she meant nothing."

"Yes or no," he said bluntly. "Just answer the damn question."

I looked away, feeling the rage burn underneath my flesh, feeling a mix of jealousy and raw pain. The thought of the two of them together, Theo pounding into her flesh and making her come, her nails deep in his back, made me want to vomit into my ashtray. "I still don't believe you. I tell you I'm about to get divorced, and the first thing you say is you want to fuck my wife?"

"Ex-wife," he said. "And based on everything you've said, you've treated her like shit. It doesn't seem like you would care if I was between her legs or not." He smashed the cigar into the glass bottom of the ashtray. "Or am I wrong?" He propped his chin on his closed knuckles and stared me down.

"Go for it. I don't give a fuck."

His stare remained glued to my face, observing me with eyes that were like a lens to a microscope. Then he reached for his glass and took a drink. "So, what's the plan with Dante?" He brushed past the awkward topic and moved on. There was no follow-up. No interrogation. He just accepted my blessing without question. "We've got to figure out who this new partner is before he makes his move. Any ideas?"

Maybe he wasn't bluffing.

"This time, we put this motherfucker in the ground."

---

I knocked on the door and waited.

A couple minutes went by, and there was no answer.

I raised my fist to knock again, but the door cracked.

Her pale face was masked in defeat. Her eyes were devoid of emotion, like she hadn't checked the peephole before she'd opened the door. When she saw me, her eyes narrowed, and a quick flash of shock hit her face, like lightning on a dark night.

I stared at her, seeing her messy bun and baggy clothes fitting poorly.

She stared back, one hand still on the door, keeping it barely cracked to bar me entry. Minutes passed, and she continued to look at me like a wild animal that had been caught by a hunter. If she didn't move, she wouldn't be noticed.

"May I come in?"

She hesitated before she gave a slight nod. Then she opened the door wide and stepped aside, her arms immediately covering her body.

I shut the door behind me then faced her.

It'd been a few days since our last conversation, and it was obvious she hadn't left the apartment or showered or probably eaten. The sight of her made my heart squeeze in pain because I knew I'd caused it and then left it to fester. "I'm sorry for being an asshole."

She tightened her arms as she took a noticeable breath.

"I just..." I had no words to describe my turmoil. It was like an avalanche that hit me all at once. It started as snowballs then turned into boulders, and then there was more than I could handle, and I was buried deep and left to suffocate. "I'm sorry for everything."

Her eyes started to water. "I'm sorry..."

She wasn't in a tight skirt and a low-cut blouse with her long hair down in curls, but she was still beautiful to me, even at her lowest. Her eyes shone with her sincerity, and I knew she felt only love for me in her heart. "I just lost it... lost my mind."

"It's okay," she said. "I forgive you."

My eyes flicked back and forth between hers. "I forgive you."

She inhaled a deep breath, the kind that made her eyes water to the point of tears. "I love you."

I finally accepted those words for the first time, let them echo in the silence as I absorbed them. When she'd said them before, I wasn't ready to hear them, but now I savored them like honey. "I love you too, baby."

———

This was no kiss. Not even an embrace. She was so self-conscious about not showering for three days or even brushing her teeth that she asked for time to get ready and present herself in a better light.

After all this time apart, all this heartache, I hardly noticed her disarray. But I wanted her to be comfortable, so I left the apartment, headed down to the pizzeria where we'd gone out together for the first time, and grabbed a pizza before I headed back.

By the time I walked back into the apartment, she was ready. Her hair was shiny and bouncy, and her pale face now had some color after she applied her blush. Her eyelashes were thick with dark makeup. In just an hour, she'd turned into a smokeshow. She glanced down at the pizza box in my hand and gave a smirk. "Some things never change."

"Nope." I set it on the counter and walked toward her, taking my time because my heart raced like a Maserati on the track. She was in a blouse and jeans, but she might as well have come out naked because I was just going to rip everything off. When we got close, I felt the rush of blood to my head, felt the tingle of excitement that she gave me the first time I saw her. There was something about this woman that made butterflies swarm in my stomach. No one else had ever made me feel that way.

As I came closer, I noticed the breath she took, the way her nerves made her eyes shift back and forth much quicker than they normally did. Her excitement was bottled, and the pressure was about to make the glass crack.

I moved into her, my arms circling her tiny waist and bringing her in close to me. I'd wanted to kiss her when I first saw her, but now that I had her in my arms, all I wanted to do was squeeze.

So I squeezed her hard.

I squeezed her against me, my chin on her head, my eyes closed. A wave of pain rushed through me as I accepted how much I'd missed her, how miserable I'd been since she'd walked out on me. She'd believed my innocence without question, but when she didn't believe my story about her father the same way, it broke me.

Her face rested against my chest, and she gripped me around the torso, her hands barely able to meet in the middle of my spine because of my bulkiness. Her quick breaths turned slow and even as the peace and joy swept through her.

I smelled her hair. Memorized the feel of her familiar body in my hands. Inhaled her perfume of roses and lavender. I wanted to stay like that forever, to have this moment last an eternity. I loved passion and excitement, but I also loved peace.

She was the first one to give it to me.

I pulled away and cupped her face, forcing her beautiful eyes on me. "It's you and me from this moment forward. Alright?"

Her eyes were locked on mine, intense in their desire but rigid in their confidence. "Yes."

"We're a family."

"I know." Her palm moved to my face, cupping my cheek. "Us versus everyone else."

My thumb brushed her bottom lip before I dipped my head and kissed her, felt those plump lips that had left invisible tattoos all over my body. Soft and full, they were exactly as I remembered...but they were even more than before.

Because now everything was different.

For the first time, there were no barriers between us, nothing keeping us apart, no threats or lies. She saw all of me, the truth in my heart, the loyalty that I'd been unable to prove.

That slow kiss intensified into something more within seconds, and soon, I was taking her entire mouth with my anxious kiss, claiming those lips the way I'd wanted to on our wedding day. My fingers slid through her soft hair that I fisted as reins. My grip was tight—and this time, I wouldn't let go.

My arms lifted her into my body, and I held her against me, our mouths still crushing together in fiery passion. My hands clutched her ass as I carried her to the unmade bed in her bedroom, and I held her there and kissed her a little longer, not wanting to break our kiss even for a few seconds when I dropped her on the bed.

I eventually rolled her to the mattress then yanked her jeans hard over her hips, tugging so hard that the fabric would have ripped if it were anything but denim. My fingers hooked into her panties too, tugging those down along with everything else. A perfectly groomed pussy was on display for me, and the sight of her glistening sex immediately made my mouth water like I was about to feast. "Forgot how pretty that pussy is..." My knees dropped to the rug underneath her bed, and my arms hooked behind her knees, spreading her open like a buffet. My lips pressed to her folds, and I was reunited with paradise, sweet and soft, the smell exactly as I remembered.

She gave a sound that was a mixture of a moan and a whimper, but it was quickly followed by the sound of my name on her eager lips. "God, Axel."

My mouth sealed around her entirely, and I gave her a hard kiss before I sucked on that little nub. I sucked harder, making her hips buck automatically, and then I swirled my tongue around her nub. Harder and harder, I pressed, cranking up the pressure, making her thighs tremble in my arms.

Her breaths deepened and quickened, and her nails started to sink into the flesh of my forearms like a spade into the dirt. Her hips began to grind, rocking into my face as those breaths turned into deep pants. "God..."

Her soft thighs squeezed my head, and she locked her ankles together around my neck before she burst, grinding into my face and moaning until her pleasure-filled cries turned into screams.

I knew there were tears without seeing her face.

I barely let her finish before I got to my feet and snapped the buttons of my jeans. I yanked everything down then pulled my shirt off quicker than I ever had. My dick was so hard, so desperate, so anxious to be inside my wife that it made my head pound.

With my boots still on my feet and my pants at my ankles, I positioned her perfectly at the edge of the bed and guided my dick inside. My cock and her pussy were like magnets, and I sank through her wetness with the speed of a bullet leaving a barrel. When I was mostly sheathed, I pushed even farther, sliding into her until there was nowhere else to go.

She gave a whimper in pain and rolled her head back, but her little hands still dug into my forearms, her nails sharp as knives.

"You like it when it hurts, baby?" I pulled back and thrust hard, hitting her deep.

She whimpered again. "Yes..."

My arms gripped the backs of her thighs and kept her legs back as I thrust, deep inside the best pussy I'd ever had, the pussy that belonged to me. At the first touch of her flesh, I was ready to go, already scorching from head to toe, already anxious to fill her pot with my seed. There'd been no one else in my bed while she was gone. There's been no other woman on my arm. My hand didn't even pay me a visit because I was either too depressed or pissed off to feel desire. So the second I was fully buried in that slit...fuck.

"Come inside me..." Her nails gripped me, her lithe body folded up like a fresh pretzel, her little pussy taking my big dick like she was an adult film star who had all the practice to handle it.

My dick gave a throb so strong, I could feel it shift inside her as I continued to slide through her sticky desire. My hips worked harder, and I pounded into her ruthlessly, making her whimper in pain and moan in pleasure, back and forth, all the way until I finished. My palms switched to the tops of her thighs, and I dragged her onto my length, buried as deep as I could go as I gave her a moan of desire.

Fuck, it felt good. So good that the world spun for a moment, that the heat inside my body broke through the surface and burned my flesh off the bone. My ass was tight and my thighs gave a tremble because the pleasure was everywhere all at once. "Baby..."

The makeup she'd just put on was a mess, the tears causing her mascara to drip from the corners of her eyes toward her ears. The foundation that masked her skin was smeared, showing the blotchiness of her cheeks. She was a crumpled mess underneath me, and she hadn't even moved a muscle —that was how good I fucked her.

I scooted her up the bed until she was in the center, several inches below where her pillows lay. My hips moved between her fleshy thighs, and they immediately squeezed me, her ankles locking together at my back.

My head dipped and I kissed her. A kiss that was slow and patient, not desperate like it'd been minutes ago. Desperation had been satisfied, and now it was time for the slow connection of our bodies, our souls.

It was time for me to make love to her.

I'd wanted to ever since she'd become my wife, but with her walls up higher than the ramparts of a castle, I could never scale them. But now, her beautiful eyes locked on mine with a sheen of vulnerability and love. Like I'd stepped back into the past, she looked at me the way she did before, like I would never hurt her. There was trust, affection, love...beauty.

I sank inside her without taking my eyes away. Instead of pushing until I felt resistance, I stopped when it felt right. I watched her inhale a deep breath when she felt me, and then her fingers buried in the back of my hair as she held my gaze.

I rocked into her, my face close to hers, my eyes mesmerized by the light in her eyes. "I love you."

Her thighs squeezed me, and her ankles tugged on me, wanting me back inside her the moment I started to pull away. Her hands moved up my chest before they cupped my face, her eyes still watery from the climax, but now wetter from the emotion. "I love you too."

# Chapter 13

## *Scarlett*

I woke up to sunlight on my face.

My drawn curtains were open a bit in the center, and the sun just happened to rise perfectly in that crack. It blanketed me with warm light, the heat enough to stir me from my sleep. But I didn't mind in the least because I didn't wake up alone that morning.

I was on my side with Axel pressed up against my back, his chest like a warm blanket against my bare skin. His arm was hooked over my waist, his hand resting on the sheets beside me. With his slow breathing, he appeared to be dead asleep.

I would have thought last night was a dream if he weren't there beside me. We shared the same pillow, shared half of the mattress and disregarded the rest. I closed my eyes again and treasured his presence, so happy that he was there with me instead of in his house on the other side of the city.

I lay there for a while, appreciating the morning rather than despising it. It was the first time I'd felt happy in weeks...maybe a month. All the chaos that had happened was distant in the rearview mirror.

I gently slipped out of bed without disturbing him, put on whatever clothes were the most easily accessible, and then crept out of the bedroom without waking him. Before we were married, I used to make him breakfast in the morning. But when I walked to the fridge, I realized I had no food.

I hadn't eaten much these last few weeks.

I quickly walked to the market, grabbed what I needed, and when I came back, he still wasn't awake. I got to work in the kitchen, making chocolate chip pancakes and apple-wood-smoked bacon, along with hashbrowns made from scratch. I'd cooked in preparation for my new restaurant, but that didn't make me happy, not like it did when I cooked for him. Lost in what I was doing, I hummed under my breath, the pans sizzling with the light coming through the uncovered windows.

"Damn, something smells good."

I nearly gave a jump when I heard his voice right behind me. I was standing at the stove over the hot pans, and I turned the burners down low before I set the spatula on the counter. When I turned to him, I expected to see his handsome and sleepy face and his messy hair, but I didn't expect to see that grin...that playful, arrogant, happy grin. I stilled when I saw it, coupled with the brightness in his beautiful eyes. I was about to ask if he was hungry, but the sight of him made me lose my train of thought.

He seemed to know my thoughts because he hooked his arm around the small of my back and pulled me in for a kiss. "I was referring to you, by the way." His hand traveled down and squeezed my ass through my jeans. He gave my ass a quick pat before he walked to the coffee machine and made himself a cup.

I stared at his muscular back as I felt a soaring sensation inside my chest. I was fully awake, fully aware of the world around me, but I felt like I was walking through a dream. Time felt different. It was slow...and easy.

He took a sip of his black coffee then turned back to me. "Can I help?"

"No. Almost done."

He carried his mug to the dining table and sat down, in nothing but his boxers, slouched in the chair in his typical *I don't give a fuck* fashion. He absent-mindedly pushed his fingers through his unkempt hair before he rested his fingers around the handle of his mug, his eyes studying me.

Once they landed on me, they stayed there, content with just watching me move about the kitchen.

I turned to the stove and got back to work.

---

We sat together at the table, the dishes between us laden with far more food than either of us could ever eat.

Just like he used to, he stacked his plate high with food and went to town, eating everything like he was starving. He gave a moan as he chewed. "This is what I'm talking about." He gave a nod in approval then took a drink of his coffee.

"I guess I haven't lost my touch."

"I think you've gotten better."

"I've been designing the menu for the restaurant."

"And it offers chocolate chip pancakes?" he teased.

"I thought I could offer brunch on the weekends."

He sliced his fork through the little cakes in preparation for another bite. "I like that idea. But you still need to cook for me—don't forget that."

I smirked as I looked down at my plate. "I won't."

We ate in comfortable silence, like we'd gone back in time to before we were married, still getting to know each other between our sexy romps on the living room couch and in the bedroom.

He wore his wedding ring, the black ring dark in comparison to his fair skin.

I'd taken mine off before I'd left. I imagined it was in his nightstand...if he hadn't thrown it away.

He wiped his plate clean, devouring everything like he hadn't eaten in weeks. It was such a contrast to my father picking one ravioli at a time and taking an eternity to finish it, or when Theo couldn't bring himself to eat more than a few bites of my cannoli. Axel ate like a starving animal... and I found that so attractive.

When he was finished, he took another drink of his coffee and sat there and stared. Stared long and hard, stared like the eye contact wasn't too intense to handle. There was no anger or resentment in his expression. It was as if I'd never left.

"I missed you." I'd missed this.

"I know, baby," he whispered. "I missed you too."

My departure had turned him into an angry maniac, but now he was back to exactly who he used to be, a man so perfect it was hard to believe he wasn't a magic trick. It was easy to forgive and forget. "Can I move back in?"

He smirked. "You think I'd let you live here?"

A hot, intoxicated blush moved to my cheeks. His affection was the best drug I'd ever had.

"Not a chance," he said. "We'll pack up when we're done with breakfast."

"I don't feel like packing." There was only one thing I felt like doing, and while it was far more exertion than packing, it was far more pleasurable.

His eyes turned confident and playful, like he knew exactly what I wanted to do instead. "I like your idea better."

---

"Did this pussy get tighter?" His hand pushed into the back of my neck, pinning my face into the rumpled sheets underneath me. My ass was in the air, and his hips thrust into me hard. "Wetter?" His fingers fisted my hair as he pinned me down, fucking me like a whore rather than his loving wife. My wrists were pinned together against my back by one of his big hands. "Prettier?"

As I started to writhe, my wrists twisted to break free, but his hold only tightened. I couldn't lift my head because I was secured in place by the mountain of his weight. Tears sprang to my eyes as incoherent moans were unleashed. "God..."

He gave a moan as I tightened around him. "That's a good girl."

My body continued to take his monster cock as pleasure exploded inside me, a high so distinct it was like surfing the clouds. Everything turned fiery hot, and I suddenly stopped caring how hard it was to breathe with my face against the sheets. It just felt so good to be fucked like this, to have a man who wanted to fuck me like this.

He came a moment later, giving a loud grunt before he shoved himself fully into me, releasing inside me as I rode the last wave of my high. Feeling him come inside me made it last a little longer, made the fire burn just a little hotter.

He finally let me go as he stepped away and headed to my bathroom to shower.

As my arms returned to my sides, I winced at the stiffness in the muscles. I was finally able to turn my head farther away from the sheets to take my first full breath. My pussy was sore from the mammoth tree trunk that had just invaded every inch, but it also burned with the aftershocks of a climax.

I finally straightened and let the stiffness ooze away. I rolled onto my side and lay there, my top still on because he'd been in too much of a rush to take his time. It was around noon, so not enough time had passed for me to want a nap, but I lay there and closed my eyes like I could drift off.

I must have fallen asleep, because Axel seemed to step out of the shower just three seconds later, dragging the towel through his short hair to dry the strands, the rest of his muscular body on display. That arrogant grin moved to his jaw. "Knocked you out cold, baby." He came to the bed then gave my ass a playful spank.

I propped myself up on one elbow to look at him, my hair a mess from the way he'd gripped it.

He dropped the towel and lay on the bed beside me, the morning light gone from the room because it was afternoon. He was propped on his elbow, looking at me with those stunning blue eyes.

"I hope our babies have your eyes." It was the first time I'd said exactly what came to mind, that I didn't censor my thoughts or feelings because I was guarded or because I didn't want him to know the depths of my affection. I just let it out...and it was nice.

Instead of that arrogant smirk, his eyes were intense, like those words were a real provocation. "Want to find out?"

"Not right now." A realization suddenly hit me like a ton of bricks. "But I haven't been taking my pill...got sidetracked."

Instead of panicking like any man would, he didn't seem to care.

"I'm sorry," I said. "I'll restart it, but you should probably wear—"

"I'm not wearing anything. And I'm not going to pull out either."

"That sounds like a dangerous game—"

"And I like danger." He smirked. "If it happens, it's a blessing. If it doesn't happen, then it'll happen later."

"You should be freaking the fuck out right now."

"You're not some woman I picked up in a bar, baby. You're my wife."

Most of my friends were excited for motherhood since they were in their early twenties, but I'd never been that way. I had other goals I wanted to achieve before I changed my life irrevocably. I wasn't looking to be a mother right now, but being the mother of his children didn't sound scary to me.

His eyes continued to watch me.

My eyes dropped to his chest, seeing the hard pecs that looked like the stone pillars that still stood in the ancient city of Pompeii.

The playfulness in his eyes started to set like the sun. "We need to figure out what to do about your father."

My eyes immediately closed, and the winter storm swept through me. Agonizing pain that had started to penetrate my mind tried to break into my body, but I continued to block the doors. "No."

"Baby—"

"Please." My eyes lifted to his. "Can we just...stay like this for a while?"

His eyes hardened in sadness as he looked at me. Seconds ticked by as the sympathy came through. "Alright...but just for a short while."

---

Axel had his men come to my apartment and gather all my things—again.

The only things left behind were the furniture and all the pots, pans, and dishes in the kitchen. It was ready for a tenant, someone who wanted to be walking distance to the market and all the nearby shops. The rental income would cover my mortgage, although I should probably consider selling it because I didn't exactly need it anymore.

When I walked back into our bedroom for the first time, it was clean and tidy, the scotch and cigars put away, the bed made like no one had slept in it since I'd been gone. I saw a prism of color coming from the nightstand, and as I approached, I realized the beauty came from my stunning wedding ring.

The ring I never should have removed.

I stared at it for a moment before I slid it onto my left ring finger and over the knuckle, aware of Axel watching me from behind.

"Better not take it off again."

When I turned around, I saw the partial smile on his lips, the affection that dimmed the resentment. "I won't." I admired it on my hand, the ring I'd missed since the moment I'd taken it off. I'd been coerced into marriage with him, but once I was his wife, it was really hard not to want to be.

---

My father had texted me multiple times asking if I wanted to talk over gelato, but I told him that I'd taken his advice and decided to give Axel another chance. This all happened through text, thankfully, because I wouldn't have been able to keep a straight face or steady my voice. He was clearly preoccupied with his plan to fuck over Axel and Theo because he accepted my explanation without further inquiry. Maybe he assumed I would go back into the honeymoon phase—or, as I suspected, he was too busy with his own coup to care.

I didn't tell Axel that he'd texted me because I was afraid the mention of him would provoke the conversation I didn't want to have, to force me to accept the horrible truth I'd ignored for so long.

It was a defense mechanism, shielding my mind from the horrible truth.

Axel and I sat across from each other in the bathtub, bottles of wine and champagne on the table Aldo had provided, and there was a pizza there as well. We'd eaten most of it, and Axel waited until I was done eating before he devoured everything left over.

"Sometimes I wonder if you actually love my cooking or you just love food."

His arms were spread over the sides of the tub as he lounged there, most of his chest exposed above the water line. "I do have a soft spot for pizza. It's the kind of food that's never bad."

"Fair," I said. "I'm glad you rehired Aldo."

"I never really fired him. After you left, I went downstairs and told him to put his stuff away."

"Good." I'd felt terrible that I was responsible for what happened. If I'd just listened to Aldo, he wouldn't have lied and gotten himself canned. "I felt so bad."

"Don't. He shouldn't have lied, especially about something like that." He grabbed his wineglass and took a drink. "I told him he would be unemployed if he ever chose to speak on my behalf that way again."

"He was probably just afraid of your reaction when I broke down your door—"

"I don't care. It's unacceptable to tell my wife I've been unfaithful when I haven't been."

That made me feel wonderful...and also shitty. "So...you weren't with anyone else?" I assumed that was the answer, but I wanted to know for certain.

His beautiful eyes suddenly turned hostile. "You have a lot of gall to ask me that."

"I assumed no, but I just wanted to—"

"You didn't assume if you had to ask," he snapped. "And no, there was no one else. There's never been anyone else since the moment you agreed to marry me."

My eyes dropped to the bubbles on the surface. "I wasn't with anyone—"

"I assumed so." His deep voice commanded me to look at him again. "That's what trust looks like."

Everything had been perfect the last two days, but now it all went to shit. "I didn't mean to offend you—"

"But you did."

"We weren't together. It's not like you would have been cheating—"

"Physically together or apart, we're together as far as I'm concerned."

"I just want to make it clear I wasn't accusing you of anything," I said. "So please stop jumping down my throat."

He looked away, grabbed his glass, and downed the rest of the contents. He returned it and stared at it a moment longer before he looked at me again. A slow breath moved into his chest and then out again. "You're right. I'm sorry."

The tightness in my chest evaporated.

"That was a hard time for me. Anytime I think about it..." He looked at the empty wineglass again.

"It's okay."

Silence trickled by, and he stared at the open bottle of wine like he was considering pouring another glass, but his mind must have been somewhere else because he didn't reach for it. "What are your plans for the restaurant?" Maybe he asked because he really wanted the answer, or maybe he just wanted to change the subject.

"Um, I kinda dropped everything this last week. But I signed a lease for that hole-in-the-wall we saw together."

He looked at me again. "I thought we agreed a bigger place was more suitable."

"The bank wouldn't give me a bigger loan than what they offered, so that was all I could afford."

"We'll cancel the lease."

"That's not how it works. I'm committed for the next year."

"That's a problem I can fix."

"How?"

"Money."

"Axel, it's fine. I don't mind opening a smaller place, and I'd rather not waste money."

"You'll waste more money running that little place and expanding later rather than doing it right from the beginning. I really think your food deserves something much grander, something that attracts the wealthy people of this city. That hole-in-the-wall place blends in with everything else on the street. It's saturated. You need something that stands out."

"I think it's fine—"

"Well, I don't," he said. "My family and I own lots of businesses throughout the city, so I know a thing or two about this sort of enterprise. Let me help you."

My arms crossed over my chest under the water.

"You wouldn't have signed that lease if things had been different."

*If my father hadn't sabotaged my life.*

He never actually said the words, but it was clear in his gaze.

I stared at the surface of the water because I knew it was coming. Could feel it in the air, the tension that was about to combust out of nothingness.

"Baby—"

"I'm not ready." I swallowed, feeling the burn in the roof of my mouth.

He stared at me in silence, his eyes flicking back and forth between mine as the seconds ticked by. He inhaled a slow breath. "I'm sorry, but you need to face it. As much as I've enjoyed this honeymoon, we have to get back to reality."

I locked my gaze on the water, fighting back the anguish that started to flood my veins. "I can't."

"You can," he said gently. "I'm here with you."

I closed my eyes for a moment before I lifted my stare.

His gaze was patient. Loving. Kind.

"I know how hard this is for you," he whispered. "I wish...I wish it weren't true."

I inhaled a shaky breath, steeling my resolve so I wouldn't raise the water level with a bucket of fresh tears.

"You have to act normal. Act like you didn't overhear that conversation. Act like I didn't tell you the truth."

"Are you fucking kidding me?" I asked incredulously. "You expect me to pull that off?"

"You *have* to pull it off."

I wasn't sure I'd ever be able to look my father in the eye again. Not after I knew the depths of his corruption. The depths of his horrible actions. "I can't believe this." My fingers slid over my mouth and cupped my lips for a second, steadying them so they wouldn't tremble. My hand returned to the warm water. "I told my father I wanted to be with you, and he still let it happen. And then I told him how miserable I was and I loved you, and he still didn't tell me the truth. He let me believe you really betrayed me."

"He said you would never speak to him again if you knew the truth, so he could never tell you."

"And he's damn right." My eyes dropped to the water again, feeling the tears coming on. "He took you away from me. He forced you to break my heart. He shot your father in the arm. He... Who knows what else he's done."

"Tried to set you up with Theo because he preferred him to me."

I hadn't believed that at first, but now it seemed entirely plausible. "I—I don't even know him. I'm not sure I ever did." I thought back to our conversations. He said I deserved a man who gave me the world, who opened doors for me, who loved me with his full heart. Axel was that man, but that wasn't the man my father wanted. The back of my head rested against the edge of the tub, and I looked toward the ceiling, feeling the tears singe the corners of my eyes. They started to drip and run down my cheeks, warm against my skin.

"Baby..."

"I can't believe he would do that to me."

"Baby." He moved across the tub to me and hooked his arms around my body before he dragged me through the water to his chest. He pulled me close and locked his arms around me like steel bars of a cage. His chest was warm, like an underwater furnace.

It was the most comfortable I'd ever been, but it still wasn't enough.

"You have me." His face pressed into the crook of my neck. "You've always had me."

# Chapter 14

## *Scarlett*

Axel walked through the building, his hand swiping across the counter at the bar. "This is it. With a little craftsmanship, we can make this place pop. A grand chandelier in the entryway, mood lighting at the bar. It's perfect."

"There have to be at least a hundred tables in here..." I looked at the behemoth of a space, empty tables sitting in an empty room.

"The kitchen supports it."

"This place is up for lease for a reason, Axel. That means someone else went under—"

"You can't compare their situation to yours."

"I'm just saying—"

"Baby, come on. It'll work out."

"What if it doesn't?"

He came back to me, a grin on his face. "Then the loss is a tax deduction. No big deal."

"I don't want to waste your money—"

"*Our* money." That searing confidence was in his eyes, looking at me with all the determination in the world. He believed in me more than anyone else ever had. "Think about it this way. I'm your silent partner. I'm investing in your business, so I get a say in the final product. This is what I envision for the restaurant. Music. Lights. Snooty waiters. This is the place. Stop thinking about the money."

"You should always think about the money."

"You know my net worth. This is nothing to me."

"Doesn't mean it should be wasted."

He rolled his eyes.

"Did you just roll your eyes at me?"

That smirk came right back. "This is what I want, and I know in your heart you want it too. So let's do this." His eyes pleaded with mine, tantalizing blue and endless in their depth. "Come on..."

My phone started to ring in my pocket, so I pulled it out and glanced at the screen.

It was my father.

My face must have immediately gone pale because Axel dropped his smile.

I didn't know what else to do, so I just let it ring.

Axel stared at me. "You can't keep avoiding him. He'll know something is up."

I let it ring, too chickenshit to answer it.

"Scarlett."

The call finally dropped.

"I can't."

A moment later, his text lit up the screen. *Call me back.*

My heart stopped aching once the dread had passed. I returned my phone to my pocket.

Axel continued to stare at me. "I know this is hard, but don't forget what's on the line."

My father-in-law's life. "I know."

"So I need you to do this for me."

"I don't know how I'll be able to maintain this façade."

Axel took in a slow breath as he considered my words. "He's a smart man. He probably already suspects something is amiss. If you think he's onto you, confront him about what you overheard. Tell him you haven't mentioned it to me because you've been so confused. That might be your opportunity to coax a confession out of him, and if it works, then you won't have to pretend anymore."

I stared at the dark marble countertop and felt my world spin. I'd never had to put on an act around my father. He was the one person I could confide all my truths to without repercussion. But now he was the person that I could trust the least. He was a complete stranger...but with my father's face.

"Text him and say you're busy with the restaurant. Ask to meet him for dinner."

"Will you come too?"

"I think it's best if I don't."

Face-to-face, one-on-one, with him sounded utterly unbearable.

"Our last conversation was quite unpleasant. And he basically hired a hit man to take me out, so he obviously doesn't care for me."

"Then I will have to confront him." Even if I never wanted to speak to him again, he'd threatened the life of my husband, and no amount of heartbreak or intimidation would let that slide. "I'll take care of it." I pulled out my phone again and typed the message without even thinking about it. *I'm caught up at the restaurant. Dinner tonight?*

His message was instantaneous, like he'd been staring at the screen waiting for my reply. *Great. See you tonight.*

I returned my phone to my pocket. "We're having dinner tonight."

Axel stared at me with his hard gaze, as if he expected me to make some kind of outburst. "You've got this."

"I'm not going to let my father hurt you."

"I don't care about him. I only care about you. And I know you can do this."

---

I arrived at the restaurant first and was taken to my father's table. My heart was in my throat like acid reflux, and my stomach was tight in uncomfortable knots. I could put up a good front when I needed to, to ignore someone's rudeness or annoyance, but to look at someone you hated like you loved them...that was impossible.

So I sat there, the anxiety flooding my blood and muscles. A basket of bread was in front of me, but it was the first time I didn't reach for a warm slice. I didn't crave wine either and left my glass untouched on the table.

Minutes trickled by, but it felt like a lifetime.

And then, finally, he entered the restaurant, in a long-sleeved hunter-green shirt and dark pants. It took him less than a second to spot me, like he'd noticed me through the window when his driver had brought him to the curb.

Once I finally saw him in the flesh, my heart stilled. Adrenaline came from nowhere and crushed me. I felt like I was about to attend a brawl, not a dinner.

He hesitated by the table, like he expected me to rise to my feet and greet him. When I didn't, he sat across from me. "Hello, sweetheart. How are you?" He pulled his chair in and looked at me with eyes that were affectionate but discerning.

How am I? Ha, if only I could answer. "Good. How about you?"

"Good?" he asked, his eyebrow cocked. "That's it?"

My heart dropped into my stomach. "What do you mean?"

"You said you and Axel got back together. I just expected more than good."

"Oh." He was right. I should have more to say. "After he took some time to calm down, he came to my apartment and said he was sorry and wanted to work on things. I've moved back in, and things have been nice. I'm sorry I've been absent...just busy."

"It's okay," he said with a smile. "I figured that was the case. I'm glad the two of you worked things out."

"Me too."

The waiter came over, and my father ordered a bottle of wine for the table, either because he expected to drink it himself or he expected me to switch my wine for his. He glanced at the menu then his hands rested together on the table. "What are you having?"

I had no appetite. "The gnocchi."

He nodded. "Same ol' salad for me."

I'd never felt so uncomfortable, so out of place with him. But I felt like there was barely enough air for us both to breathe. Or we were both in the desert, but he was the only one with water. I couldn't start a conversation or ask a question, not when my mind was elsewhere.

He continued to look at me. "Everything alright?"

"Yes," I said quickly. "How are things with you?"

"Just working on a few projects."

"How did that meeting go?" I asked.

"What meeting?"

"You had someone at the house when I stopped by."

"Oh, that's right." He watched the waiter fill his glass before he took a drink. "Yes, it was an old friend. Just catching up."

"If he's an old friend, wouldn't he have understood that your daughter needed you?" I was supposed to be calm. I was supposed to be sly. But shit was about to hit the fan because I'd inherited his temper.

His eyes narrowed on my face. "So you are angry with me..."

I'd just stepped into the snake pit without gloves or boots.

"Considering everything worked out between you two, I assumed you wouldn't be upset—"

"I forgot my purse." The moment of truth had arrived—and we hadn't even ordered dinner. "I sat in the car for a while fighting back tears, but when I tried to drive away, I realized I had no keys. So I came back in to grab it."

My father was still and composed, but his eyes darted back and forth between mine.

"You asked this *old friend* to kill my husband." I wanted it to be a misunderstanding, but what possible misunderstanding could there be? I'd heard him, like a boom box in a silent room, and there was no mistaking the threat.

He gave no reaction to this. None whatsoever. He just continued his stare. He didn't feign surprise or look appalled by the accusation. But he didn't admit to it either, plotting his next move behind the rough exterior. "You were eavesdropping—"

"I forgot my purse. And even if I were maliciously and intentionally eavesdropping, it doesn't change what you said. You said you would kill both Axel and Theo. Axel, my husband, and Theo, my brother-in-law. You said those words."

He inhaled a slow breath, not blinking once since the accusation had been put on the table.

The waiter approached. "What will we be ordering—"

"Leave us, and don't come back." My father didn't raise his voice or drop it, but there was a distinct threat to his tone.

The waiter remained for a moment, taking a second to wonder if he had heard my father correctly, but whether he did hear correctly or not, the tension between us was unmistakable, so he fled.

My father continued his ruthless stare, all the fatherly affection he'd previously held gone. "Scarlett, you had just told me he served you divorce papers—"

"And five minutes later, you decided to kill him?" I couldn't believe he tried to justify it, let alone admit it.

"Those plans must have already been planted in your head and grown to a full tree for you to act on it so suddenly."

He stared, his features those of my father, but his spirit belonging to someone I didn't recognize. "You aren't even denying it."

"Because I wouldn't lie to you."

"Really?" I snapped. "So, once he was dead, how would you explain it?"

"Nothing happened, so we don't need to discuss this further—"

"I told you he was the love of my life—and you plotted to kill him. So yes, something *did* happen."

"I told you I've never liked him—"

"It doesn't matter what you think. I love him. I'm in love with this man."

He didn't look guilty or apologetic. He was a man without a conscience. "He went to prison—"

"He's innocent."

"He cheated on you."

I sucked in a hard breath and swallowed, using my full restraint to keep my mouth shut. My eyes burned as my eyelids were stretched open, and my rage was restrained in a delicate glass bottle that was about to shatter.

He waited for my rebuttal.

But I couldn't give it.

"He's never been good enough for you—"

"So he deserves to die?"

"He backstabbed me—"

"Because you backstabbed him first. What the fuck is wrong with you?" Now my voice rose in complete disregard to the people enjoying their dinner around us. "How dare you." There were no words to match my anger, no words that could convey the depth of my rage. "Axel doesn't like you either, but he would never *kill* you. Who are you? Who the fuck are you?"

The hardness in his face started to slacken. "Sweetheart—"

"Don't sweetheart me, asshole."

"Axel made some bad decisions that really messed up my business—"

"I was almost raped and killed, and the only reason I wasn't was because of him."

"That meeting wouldn't have happened in the first place if Axel had any business sense—"

I shoved my chair back and got to my feet.

"Scarlett."

"Fuck off." I stormed off, leaving him to foot the bill for our wine. It would give me a chance to escape.

But he walked out right behind me and onto the sidewalk. "Scarlett."

I walked down the sidewalk and headed to my car, which was parked in a lot a block over. My jacket had been left on the back of the chair, so I walked in the cold, but my anger created an inferno of warmth inside me.

"Stop." He grabbed my arm and pulled me back. "Let me explain—"

"Explain what?" I snapped. "How can you explain this? Who was the guy you were with, and why would he want to kill your business partners?"

"Have you told Axel this?"

"Is that all you care about?"

"No," he said with a cold voice. "But I don't want him getting a false version of the truth—"

"I didn't say anything to him because I hoped, *prayed*, that I didn't overhear what I thought I heard. I didn't want my father and my husband to pull out their guns and start shooting each other."

He raised his hand. "Then let's forget the whole thing."

"Forget?" I asked incredulously. "You think I can just forget this?"

"No harm was done."

"Trust me, it was done," I hissed. I turned away again.

"Sweetheart, please. It's complicated."

"It's not complicated." I turned back to him. "If I hadn't been in the right place at the right time, my husband would be dead a few days from now."

"I wouldn't have gone through with it once I knew you were back together—"

"You expect me to believe that?"

"I've never lied to you before, sweetheart."

I was repulsed. Utterly repulsed. I believed my father had forced Axel to hurt me, but I always hoped that there was more to the story, that perhaps something got lost in translation. But hearing my father openly admit this...made me realize it was completely true. Every word that Axel said. "Really?" I asked. "*Never?*"

His steely eyes hardened.

"I'm not sure I can believe that."

"Axel has complicated my business, has compromised my relationship with the Colombians, a relationship I've cultivated for the last twenty years—"

"We sat together in that restaurant, and I asked you if you had anything to do with my breakup with Axel. You looked me in the fucking eye and said no. Was that the truth?"

My father froze in place, his stare guarded by a twelve-foot wall.

"You're trying to get rid of him now. What if you were trying to get rid of him then? You didn't care about making me a widow. Why would you care about making me heartbroken?" My eyes took in the immovable features of his face, piercing the stone of his eyes. My breaths were quick, and I felt the dump of adrenaline in my blood. I wasn't sure if I wanted to run or slam my fit into his face. "Did you lie to me?"

He retained his silence, only breathing, his eyes vicious.

I knew there would be no answer, so I turned my back on him and walked off.

He let me go.

When I returned home, Axel was on the couch in front of the TV screen. He didn't seem to be watching anything, just staring at the screen as he waited for me to return from the dinner. His head snapped my way the second I walked into the room, and then he was on his feet. He didn't ask how I was. He figured it out on his own, eyes switching back and forth between mine as he gauged my mood.

"He admitted it." I tossed my purse on the table and kicked off my heels until I was on my bare feet. "Even tried to justify it. Said he thought it didn't matter because we were getting a divorce." I dropped into one of the armchairs at the dining table and slouched, my elbow on the table with my fingers underneath my chin.

Axel pulled one of the chairs close to me and sat down.

"I—I don't even know him."

His hand moved to mine on the table.

"I've never known him..."

He didn't gloat. Didn't say I told you so. There was no victory in his eyes.

"Then I asked him if he'd pulled this kind of stunt in the past...and he didn't own up to it. I asked him if he'd lied to me when I looked him dead in the eye and asked if he'd said something to you to make you go away."

"What did he say?"

"Nothing."

"I doubt he'll ever admit that. Plotting to kill me is more forgivable than that."

I stared at his hand as it rested on mine, his wedding ring sitting there. "I don't know him. I've never known him." He'd lied to my face, and then a moment later, Axel had walked in with Cassandra, an invisible gun pointed at his head. My father had planned all of that, planned for me to be utterly heartbroken just because he didn't like Axel. "I feel so stupid..." Tears welled in my eyes and streaked down my cheeks. "Everything you said about him...you were right. I could have lost you for good and continued to eat his bullshit for the rest of my life."

"But you didn't," he whispered. "Nothing will come between us again."

"I was fucking livestock for him this entire time. I was running around in a little pen, eating slop from the damn trough. He's never given a damn about me. He hates you enough to break us up, but he didn't hate me enough to guilt me into marrying you once that suited him. I hate him."

Axel's fingers dug into mine as he held my hand on the table. Silence trickled by as the echo of my words filled the air. "I don't like your father. Never have and never will. But I do believe he cares about you."

My eyes lifted to his.

"In fact, I know he does. He just has a strange way of showing it."

"You're seriously defending him right now?"

"I'm not defending him. I just want you to know that he does care for you. He's lied to you and manipulated you, and he's done unforgivable things, but he does love you. I know this in my heart."

I pulled my hand away from his.

Axel took a slow breath at my rejection.

My arms folded over my chest, and I sat against the back of the chair. My phone was in my back pocket, and I'd expected it to vibrate and ring nonstop, but my father hadn't tried to contact me. He was probably plotting his next move, a trick I wouldn't fall for.

"What can I do?"

My eyes returned to his. "Nothing. There's nothing anyone can do."

"Did you eat dinner?"

I shook my head. "We barely had a sip of wine."

"I can take you out for pizza."

"I'm not hungry."

"Want to take a bath?"

"No. I think I just want to go to sleep." That was what I did when I was depressed. My mind turned off, and all I did was rest. I'd been down so low just a week ago, and now I was in a new era of sadness. Could I just be happy... for a little while?

Axel looked like he wanted to argue, to make me eat dinner or relax in his arms, but he let me be. "Then let's go to bed."

I went into the bathroom and did my nighttime routine, washing my face and brushing my teeth, but I barely looked in the mirror, like I didn't want to see my own features. I pulled my hair back in a bun, and then I returned to the bedroom.

Axel was in bed, the sheets to his waist, one arm propped under his head.

I pulled back the covers and got in bed beside him. My back was to him, and I stared at the curtains that were closed over the window.

He moved against me, his chest against my back, and he tightened his arm around my waist and pulled me close, his face pressed into the back of my hair. It was only eight thirty, far too early for bed, but I didn't have the energy to do anything but lie there. My phone was left in the other room, so if it rang, I wouldn't have to hear it.

"I love you, baby."

Despite my heartache, I still melted at those words. "I love you too."

# Chapter 15

## *Axel*

Scarlett wanted to be alone, to mope in the bedroom by herself, sometimes on the couch and sometimes in the tub. There was nothing I could do for her, so I went back to my routine, working out in the morning and then overseeing my businesses throughout the day. Now that Scarlett and Dante weren't speaking, I didn't involve myself in the business at all because I wasn't sure where I stood anymore.

I should be happy that Scarlett was my wife again, that she'd seen her father for the snake that he was, but I actually felt like shit. It was the kind of pain that she would never conquer, a mark that would blemish her skin for the rest of her life, and I hated that. What had happened with my parents...I wouldn't wish that on anyone else.

In the evening, I was on the couch in the living room, and she was in the tub with a bottle of wine. We hadn't said much to each other all day. It ruined me to hold my silence, but my comfort would only suffocate her.

My phone vibrated, and I saw a text from Aldo. *Dante is here to see Scarlett.*

I'd known Dante would make his move at some point, and I'd asked Aldo to be quiet about it, rather than coming straight to the bedroom door.

*How would you like me to handle this?*

*Escort him to the parlor. I'll be there shortly.* I walked into the bedroom and saw the cracked door to the bathroom, the candlelight shifting and moving on the ceiling. I pulled on a shirt and left the bedroom, closing the door so quietly she wouldn't know I'd left. Then I headed downstairs to the parlor, seeing the fire in the hearth, the tray of cigars and scotch, and the man sitting in the armchair, looking pale as a ghost.

I stared at him for a moment before I moved to the opposite armchair.

He wouldn't look at me. Not in disdain...but something else.

I sat there and waited for him to ask for Scarlett.

He didn't. "I was expecting you." He sank back in the armchair and met my gaze head on.

My ankle rested on the opposite knee, my closed fist against my cheek. "She doesn't know you're here."

"I figured as much."

I rubbed my fingers across my jawline, seeing the darkness that had invaded his soul. There was no hardness to his stare, no arrogance to his stature. He seemed dead on the inside, defeated in the very war he'd started. "What do you want?"

He stared at the table between us, his fingertips rubbing against his temple. "To speak with my daughter...but I suspect that's not going to happen. She's ignored all my calls and texts."

"I'm not keeping her from you—if that's what you're wondering."

He looked at me once more. "I'm sure if she did want to see me, you would keep her away from me."

"I don't tell Scarlett what to do. She makes her own decisions. You should take a page from my book."

A slight smirk moved on to his lips. "The first insult of the night."

"I can ask her to come down, but I suspect she'll say no."

He gave a heavy sigh. "I need to speak to her. I have to make this right."

"I don't know if you can make this right, Dante. It's too much shit for her to forgive. She looks at your relationship through an entirely new lens. Every word you've ever said, she's picked apart with a comb."

"Did you tell her, then?"

"Tell her what?"

He looked at me full on. "You know what."

"I didn't have to tell her, Dante."

He stared for several seconds, his gaze hard as stone.

"You fucked yourself over when she heard what you said. Don't blame me for that."

He looked away.

"So?"

His eyes came back.

"Still going to pull the trigger?" If his answer was yes, I'd kill him right there. I had a gun strapped underneath my armchair. In light of everything that had happened, I knew Scarlett would understand.

"Not really much point, is there?" He looked at the fire and slouched in the chair, like he didn't want to be there but had nowhere else to go.

I actually felt bad for him.

"She'll never forgive me." He spoke so quietly, his words were barely audible. "I don't even know why I bothered coming down here."

"Who was that meeting with?"

He turned back to me.

"The man who agreed to take out Theo and me."

"It doesn't matter." He looked at the fire again. "I've called the whole thing off."

"How do I know you're not lying?"

"There may be a chance my daughter forgives me...someday. But she'll never forgive me if you die and she knows I'm the one responsible. I've dissolved our partnership and told him we wouldn't be moving forward."

"I should kill you, you know that?"

"My daughter wouldn't appreciate that. And if she really didn't care...then I wish I were dead." He spoke with a breathlessness, like he was too tired to carry on this conversation. It was a very different version of him than I'd ever met.

"That was a stupid move, Dante."

He gave a sigh. "I just wanted my business back. Theo had great connections, but you're a young hothead who lets his arrogance get in the way."

"You're one to talk."

He didn't rise to the insult, still not caring. "Doesn't matter anymore."

I let the silence settle in, pierced by the crackle of the flames every few seconds. There was nothing left to discuss, but he continued to linger, like his daughter would come around the corner at any moment. "Dante."

After a breath, he looked at me.

"I only took your business because you took Scarlett. I never would have wanted it if you'd just let us be together."

He gave an almost imperceptible nod. "I know. A mistake I'll always regret."

"So I'd like to give it back to you—as a sign of a truce."

The defeat in his eyes started to fade as light returned to his stare. "A truce..."

"I know what it's like not to have a relationship with my parents. I don't want that for Scarlett. Despite the horrible things you've done, I know you love your daughter. You just have a really fucked-up way of showing it."

In disbelief, he continued to stare.

"I can ask Theo to walk away too. He would do that for me."

Dante seemed to be stunned into silence because he didn't speak for a long while. "While I'm touched by your merciful offer, it doesn't matter now. I lost the one thing that actually matters."

"I'll help you rebuild this broken relationship, Dante. As I said before, I think it would be a great disservice to her to lose her father. Your business will be separate from your personal relationship with Scarlett, whom you need to accept will never be associated with that world again. And you need to tell her the truth. The whole truth. Everything."

He released a shaky breath.

"Tell her—and I will do everything I can to help you."

"You said she already knows—"

"But it should come from you. And you should explain why you made the decisions that you did. She'll still be angry, but at least she'll understand why you did those horrible things. With the full story, she'll never have to wonder, and she'll be able to move forward with life— forward with you."

He looked away. "Why would you help me?"

"I just told you—"

"We both know I'm the reason your family hates you." He said it quietly, with a hint of shame. "How can you forgive me for that—"

"Who said I forgive you?" I snapped. "I will never forgive you for shoving my father to the floor and shooting him in the arm. I will never forgive you for threatening my mother. I will never forgive you for destroying what little hope I had of reconciliation. But this isn't about me. It's about Scarlett. I can put aside my own feelings for her best interests—because that's what a husband does."

He blinked several times as he stared at me. "I guess I was wrong about you."

"Yeah, you were."

"I'm sorry for all the complications I caused to your relationship. But it seems like this love is real. Otherwise, it wouldn't have endured for so long. That's a special kind of love."

It is.

"How much space does she need before I try to talk to her?"

"There's not enough space in the world, Dante. But I can bring her down here now."

"You think she'll talk to me?"

"I can encourage her."

He gave a nod. "I would deeply appreciate it if you did."

———

I walked into the bathroom and found her in the tub, the bubbles to her chest, her skin wet and glistening. She'd be the sexiest thing I'd ever seen if her eyes weren't so hollow. "You drank all the wine."

"Aldo needs to bring two bottles next time."

I sat on the edge of the tub. "One bottle is cute. Two is not so cute."

"You're one to talk." Her eyes were slightly playful.

"Your father is downstairs." I didn't know how to address the situation because there was no easy way to do it. I knew how it would provoke her, but using a butter knife instead of a steak knife wouldn't make it hurt less.

She reacted exactly as I expected, turning still with guarded eyes.

"I think you should talk to him."

"Why?"

"There're things that need to be said."

"I don't think there's anything worth saying."

"Scarlett, I understand you're angry—"

"I thought you hated him."

"I do."

She raised her hands in confusion. "Then why would you want me to talk to him?"

"Because he's your father. And I'd give anything to talk to mine."

Her hands lowered, and the anger in her eyes dimmed. "The situations are not comparable—"

"The details don't matter. I would just hate for you to live the life I've led."

"I thought you would be happy to have him out of our lives."

"All I've ever wanted is you. I can tolerate him forever as long as we're together. That was never the issue. It became the issue when he took you away from me. But now he can't do that again, so he's not a threat to me. As far as I'm concerned, our beef is squashed."

"He was going to try to kill you—"

"A lot of people have tried to kill me. It's nothing personal."

She stared at me for several seconds, like she couldn't believe I'd just said that.

"Get out and talk to him."

She remained under the water in the tub, the defeat in her eyes. "I'm not going to forgive him—"

"I didn't ask you to. No one expects you to. But we both know this conversation is going to happen at some point. May as well do it now while he's here." I got to my feet and gave her my hand. "Come on, baby."

She hesitated before she rose out of the tub, water dripping over her luscious curves, and she took my hand as I helped her step over the side.

I wrapped her tight in a towel and pressed a kiss to her temple.

"I want you there too." Her arms were pinned inside the cotton, with her wet hair stuck to the back of her neck. Small and vulnerable, she looked so precious to me.

"Yeah?"

She nodded.

"Alright. Get dressed."

When we walked into the parlor, Dante's eyes immediately went to Scarlett.

It was as if I wasn't even there.

His defeated and empty gaze was suddenly bright with affection...and hard with despair. He rose out of his chair slowly to greet her, like there would be a chance for a hug, but she stayed on the other side of the coffee table.

I moved to a chair in the corner of the room, present but out of the way.

She sat down in the armchair.

He slowly lowered himself back down, his ass right at the edge, looking at Scarlett like he couldn't believe she was really there.

Her hair was still damp because she hadn't dried it, just squeezed it with a towel so the drops stopped falling on the floor. She'd put on a pair of jeans she'd left on the floor of the closet and pulled on a hoodie. Despite the warmth from her long bath, her cheeks were pale as if she was freezing cold.

Dante continued to stare at her like she was an angel sent from the heavens. "Thank you for seeing me."

Her hands were together on her lap, and her back didn't touch the chair, as if she expected this conversation to be so brief there was no point in getting comfortable. "You can thank Axel because I had no interest in coming down here." She stared at the coffee table between them, like meeting his gaze was simply too painful.

Dante was quiet for a while, swallowing that rejection like a big pill. "Well, I appreciate it, nonetheless."

Silence passed. A lot of it.

I looked at Dante then looked at Scarlett.

Dante cleared his throat. "I came here tonight to apologize to you. I'm so sorry for everything. I want you to know that you're the single most important thing in the world to me, and I'm sorry that I've made you feel otherwise."

She stared at the table like those words meant nothing to her. "Actions speak louder than words. You were going to kill Axel if I hadn't overheard you. Forgetting my purse is the reason he still breathes." She lifted her chin and looked at him.

"You said you were divorcing."

"Again, what does that matter? I told you I loved him."

Now Dante broke eye contact because her savagery was too much.

"You're the reason he left me." Her anger died and slowly turned to sadness, like she was remembering that heart-break. "You let me believe that he...he left me for someone else. You have no idea how that fucked me up."

Dante didn't look at her again.

"You can't sit there and say you care about me, not after that."

Dante took a breath before he looked at his daughter again. "He went to prison for assault and rape—"

"I told you he was innocent."

"I wanted to protect you. I told you from the beginning I didn't like him, but then you snuck around behind my back. I told Axel to go away, but he didn't listen to me either. As horrible as it is, I thought you deserved better. The execution was horrible and probably caused more damage than it prevented, but I knew you deserved someone better."

"Someone better..." She released a painful chuckle. "There is no one better."

A twinge of warmth moved through my chest.

"You're right," Dante said. "Axel is a fine man with admirable qualities. Over time, he's proven to me how much he adores you. All I ever wanted is for a man to love you more than himself...and he definitely loves you more than anything."

"Did you realize this before or after you plotted to kill him?" she snapped.

"Before," he said honestly. "You need to understand that all I've wanted is my business, and Axel crossed me when he took it. I'm not the kind of man to accept defeat. My decision had nothing to do with your relationship—"

"Which means my relationship didn't matter. Which means that I'm not the single most important thing to you. Your business is." Her ferocity burned like a wildfire. "Always has been and always will be."

Dante released a barely contained grimace.

"How could you hurt me like that?" Now the ferocity was gone, replaced by raw pain. "You knew he was going to walk into that restaurant with her. You knew I was going to see it and die. You knew...you knew all of it. For months, you watched me suffer and said *nothing*. You set me up with Theo when I'd already found someone I wanted to be with."

"I didn't know you felt so strongly—"

"Bullshit. You knew. And then when Axel took your business right from underneath you, you asked me to marry him to get it back. The very man you'd taken away. Now that it suited you, you suddenly had a change of heart. If Axel hadn't done everything in his power to get me back, he would have ended up with someone else and I would have ended up with the lesser choice. How can you live with that?"

His head was bowed in shame.

"There is no coming back from this. I want you out of my house—and out of my life."

Dante lifted his chin to display his face, and that's when the tears were visible. His eyes were wet and glistened in the glow of the fireplace. "Sweetheart—"

"Don't sweetheart me." She kept her voice strong, but her eyes were purposely elsewhere, like she couldn't see him like this, no matter how angry she was. That meant she cared...she still cared. "Please go."

He remained in the chair, blinking several times to dispel the burn in his eyes. "There must be something I can do—"

"If you're really sorry, you'll leave me alone and never bother me again."

The words made him flinch, made him suck in a harsh breath and blink several more times. "I promise I will never do anything like this again—"

"It's not about a repeat offense." She looked at him again. "It's the fact that the entire time, when I thought we were so close, I was just your fucking puppet. You were never going to give me the business, were you? You were just using me to marry me off to someone powerful so you could grow your alliances."

"You were never my puppet, Scarlett," he said. "I just got lost in all the bullshit. I got lost in the money and the power. The only thing that actually matters is the two of us...and I somehow forgot that."

Her arms tightened over her chest.

"I worked so hard when you were little because I wanted to provide for you. I wanted you to have a better life than I did, the four of us sleeping in a single bedroom. But I took that too far, lost sight of why I was doing all of this, let my good intentions mold into something entirely new and terrible. I know I've done awful things, and I'm honest about that. But never once have I not loved you." His tears started to break through the cracks in his armor. He struggled to look at his daughter, who continued to give him the cheek. "Axel is right. Family is everything. Give me another chance."

"This family is toxic, manipulative, and conniving." When she looked at him again, it was with the same coldness.

"And I want no part of it." She got to her feet. "Did my mother actually not want me, or was that a lie?"

Dante couldn't hide the hurt the question provoked.

"Did you kidnap me, and she's been looking for me all this time?"

He bowed his head and let her question hang in the air between them.

Scarlett turned away and walked out of the room. Didn't wait for me to join her.

Dante remained there and slid forward, catching his face on his palms as his elbows rested on his knees. His fingers pushed through his hair, and he gave a painful sigh. And in the light of the fireplace, I saw a tear fall.

I should have felt nothing. Nothing at all. But...I felt sad.

He took a moment before he righted himself and sniffed loudly. He wiped his face on his sleeve and took in a hard breath. His cheeks were full of crimson, and his eyes burned from the inflammation of his sinuses.

I moved to the couch and took a seat. "Give her some time."

He rubbed his palms together and composed himself, hiding his weakness from me. "She's right. What I've done...is unforgivable."

"I agree."

He turned his head slightly to look at me.

"But love doesn't care about forgiveness. Love doesn't care about anything. That's why it's love."

———

I didn't mention her father again.

Their conversation put her in a depressive state for a few days, and once she was out of it, I didn't want to put her back in the hole. I gave her time to breathe, to enjoy the spring sunshine that started to flood the city.

I sat at the kitchen island and watched her work. Her thick hair was pulled back in a bun while she wore leggings and a sports bra with her athletic jacket slipping halfway down, showing most of her stomach.

She sauteed the dish for a few more minutes before she transferred it to two plates. She placed one in front of me along with a fork. "This is the last entrée. Assuming we like this, our menu is complete."

Steam wafted from the dish like smoke from a blazing fire, but I was so eager for a bite that I stabbed my fork into the food and took a bite.

"You can let it cool."

"I'm hungry." I ignored the heat and chewed, letting the sauce and flavors all come together. "Fuck yes, this is going on the menu."

"Are you sure? Because you've never vetoed any of my dishes."

"I said no to that gorgonzola fig thing."

"Yes, because it was a salad."

I took another bite. "Baby, everything you make is good. If you weren't my wife, I'd be eating there every night, trying to make you my wife."

An involuntary blush moved to her cheeks as the smile tugged at her lips.

"I'd eat your food then that pretty pussy."

"Wow..." She took a bite of her own food. "At least we aren't in public right now."

Without waiting for my meal to cool, I ate it all, wiping the plate clean with a piece of bread. "Our menu is complete. Now we need to set up with the vendors, add some décor, and hire staff."

"Yes, the hard part."

"I think the menu would be the hard part for most people."

"Not me. It's the only part I like."

Aldo came into the kitchen. "Theo is here to see you, sir."

"Bring him in."

A moment later, Aldo escorted Theo into the room. He wore a short-sleeved black shirt and jeans, already dressing for the warmth of the beginning of spring. "Something smells good."

"Hope you're hungry." Scarlett plated a dish and set it at the bar beside him.

"I can always eat." Theo took the seat beside me, and just as I did, he ignored the steam and jumped in headfirst. "It's good."

She poured him a glass of wine then started to clean the kitchen.

"We're done making the menu," I said. "Now we have to do all the other shit. Vendors, dishes and silverware, staff, all that stuff."

"That shouldn't be hard for you."

"The first thing we need to do is hire a manager with experience so they can be part of this process."

"Not a bad idea," Theo said. "But you aren't getting mine."

I smirked. "I would never."

Theo wiped his plate clean, and Scarlett carried it to the sink. When her back was turned, he addressed me. "We need to talk."

"I knew this conversation was coming." I raised my voice and looked at Scarlett. "We'll be back, baby."

"Alright." She tipped the pan and placed all the leftovers in the glass container to save for later.

Theo and I walked into the parlor, where the fire was cold and the coffee table was empty. He dropped down into his usual chair and cut straight to the chase. "What's the plan?"

"About what?"

He cocked his head slightly. "Dante plans to kill us, and we have no retaliation?"

I knew Theo was a no-nonsense, no-second chances kind of guy, so this wouldn't go down easy. "I spoke to Dante. He said he called off the partnership. He also informed the Colombians there would be no deal."

"And you believe him?" he asked with a sneer.

"Absolutely."

Theo rubbed his palms together in his annoyance. "What's going on with him and Scarlett?"

"He apologized, but she wants him out of her life."

"Smart girl."

"I think that might feel right in the moment, but a few years down the line, she'll feel differently. Our children won't have a single grandparent. Her anger will soften into longing and regret. I don't want that for her."

"After all the shit he did?" he asked incredulously.

"I know he's an asshole, but I know he loves her."

Theo shook his head in disappointment. "I couldn't agree less, but this is your life, not mine."

"I just want the best for Scarlett."

"If you say so..." He sat back in the chair and rested his ankle on the opposite knee. "We should remove Dante from the business. He'll probably throw a fit, so we'll just remind him it's a better alternative than being hung in his closet."

I almost couldn't bring myself to do it, to face Theo's disappointment after all the help he'd given me. "We both know I only took the business from him to get Scarlett back. Now that I have her, I'm not that interested in it anymore."

He took in that information with a hard stare, his arms on the armrests. "If your heart's not in it, don't worry about it. I suspected this might happen now that you've settled down. Pretty soon, she's going to leg-lock you to get that baby."

"Leg-lock?"

"It's when a woman locks her ankles together so you can't pull out."

"And has that happened to you?" I asked with interest.

He gave a shrug but never answered.

"I've decided to do more than just step aside from the business. I've decided to give it back to him."

Theo cocked his head, a flash of rage in his eyes. "You did what now?"

"It's important to him, and it means nothing to me."

"And what about me? What about all the work I've put into this?"

"I won't make you do anything, Theo. But it would be nice to agree to a truce and move on with our lives."

"You may have settled down with a woman, and her father may have come to his senses, but my life hasn't changed. To let go of this business would be a mistake. The Skull Kings would never accept my giving away a business they worked on and just handing it over without real justification."

I hadn't expected such a disagreement about this. "Would you be willing to work with Dante going forward?"

"After he plotted to kill me?" He laughed, a cold, uproarious laugh. "The only reason he's breathing is because of you. That's the most mercy I'll grant him. What he should do is hand the business to me and bow out."

"If he doesn't get Scarlett back, he'll have nothing left."

"Boo-hoo. You think I give a shit? Why do you give a shit?"

"With me out of the picture and everything that's happened with Scarlett, I think Dante would be a good business partner. We haven't seen his professional qualities because we've been too busy fighting each other, but he is a smart businessman. I'm sure you guys could turn over a new leaf and start fresh."

"I don't trust him."

"I didn't ask you to trust him. I was always the thorn in his side, but now I'm gone, so there's no reason for you to have issues. He wanted to work with you all along, so you're the business partner he wanted in the first place. Just put aside your differences and make money."

He relaxed into the chair and rested his hand on his knee. "It looks like you relaxed...and pulled your head out of your ass. I was just about to ask her to dinner too..." He smirked, like this was just some fun game.

"You want to die, motherfucker?"

"Come on," he said with a laugh. "I did you a favor."

"By trying to fuck my wife?"

"By reminding you of all the men who *will* want to fuck your wife. How long was it before you went over there?"

I ignored his stare and his question.

He smirked. "I bet it was five minutes."

"New subject."

"You're welcome, asshole." He looked around the parlor. "You got any booze or what? Where are the cigars? Clean air makes me sick."

# Chapter 16

## *Scarlett*

It'd been a few weeks since I'd seen my father.

Axel didn't mention him. Didn't try to talk me into calling or texting. It was nice not to think about it, to put it out of my head and just live my life. My father didn't contact me either...and that was a bit of a surprise.

I walked into the restaurant and found Axel on top of the bar, working on the pendant lights positioned over the surface. He was in jeans and a long-sleeved shirt, the sleeves pushed up to his elbows. There was debris on the countertop.

"What are you doing?" I asked.

"The contractor put the lights on a switch, when I specifically asked for a dimmer."

"So...you're doing what?"

"Switching it to a dimmer."

"You—you know how to do that?"

He wiped the sweat from his forehead then looked down at me. "Baby, I know how to do a lot more than eat and fuck." He tightened the screws again then hopped off the counter to test the switches. "There we go." The lighting turned bright then dark again, on a spectrum of intensity. "What do you think?"

I took a look around, seeing how much we had accomplished in a short amount of time. It was dark and chic, black marble with white streaks, definitely a sexy vibe. "It's stunning. Had no idea you had such good taste."

He came to me, that smirk on his face, and then gripped me around the small of my back and pulled me in for a kiss. "Why do you think I picked you?" In the middle of the kiss, he gave my ass a squeeze. "I have damn good taste." That boyish grin was on his face as he pulled away and looked at me. "You got the menus?"

I was in a sort of daze whenever he kissed me like that, whenever he sprinkled me with affection that made my blood burn my cheeks. All the time we lost during our separation was such a waste, but at least we had what we'd always wanted now. It took me a second to shake it off before I pulled the folder from my purse. I opened the folder and showed him the document on thick cream paper.

He read it over. "Meatball lollipops...those are my favorite." He continued to read down. "Scallops...ratatouille...I'm starving." He turned the page and looked over the wine list. "It all looks great. I'd eat all of this."

"I know, babe."

He lifted his head from the menu and looked at me, a massive grin on his face.

"What?"

"You called me babe."

"Oh." I'd barely called him that since the first time we were together. It might have slipped out sometimes after we got married. But it'd been restrained most of the time, the affection refusing to leave my body.

"I like it when you call me that." He gave my ass a squeeze and yanked me close, pressing a hard kiss to my mouth as an act of ownership. "Let's finish up here so we can go home. I want that pussy on my face." He gave my ass a smack before he walked off and headed into the kitchen.

"What do you think about Alessandra?" He sat across from me at a table in the restaurant, her résumé on the surface between us.

"She seems nice."

"I don't care if she's nice. Her résumé says she has a lot of experience. Worked at a lot of good restaurants in the city." He pulled the résumé close and glanced at it again. "I think she'd be a great person to hire all the staff and oversee everything leading up to the opening of the restaurant. You don't want to worry about all those details all the time. I don't either. I'm a busy man with lots of shit to do."

"Busy man, huh?" I teased.

"You know I own lots of different businesses."

"You're sure home a lot..."

"Would you rather I be gone all the time?"

"Not what I'm saying."

"And by having her run the restaurant, you can be home with me. Why do things the hard way when you can do things the smart way? When we have a family, you're going to be grateful for the help. And right now, you can focus on what you do best—the food."

"You make a sound argument."

"I'm a very smart man, baby."

I chuckled.

"What was that?"

"Nothing."

He leaned forward in his chair, his elbows resting on the table. "You want me to fuck you right here on this table?"

"We're right by a window."

"You think I care?" The playfulness was gone, and he stared me down like he was the hawk and I was the prey.

I looked down at her resume. "Let's hire Alessandra. That means we should be able to open in two weeks."

Axel didn't say anything.

I met his look again.

He still wore the same expression as he did before.

"We aren't doing that here—"

"Yes, we are." He rose out of his chair then came around the table and grabbed the back of my chair. Then he pulled it across the hardwood floors, dragged it to the other side of the restaurant where there wasn't a window. Comfy couches were placed against the walls, underneath the chandelier, where people could comfortably wait for their table.

"What if someone walks in?"

"The door is locked, and we're closed for business." He got me out of the chair then guided me to the black velvet couch, the chandelier glowing above us. He pulled off my boots then tugged at my jeans, getting me naked from the waist down. Then he dropped his pants, bringing them just below his ass. He moved on top of me, warm between my thighs, and pushed through my tightness and then sank in.

I sucked in a harsh breath through my teeth at the forceful entrance, but then I moaned the rest of the way, loving the feeling of his fat dick inside me. Whoever said size didn't matter was full of horseshit. His big dick hurt sometimes, but damn, it felt incredible.

He released a sexy moan when he was fully sheathed, holding himself above me on those muscular arms, claiming me in the new restaurant that he'd bought for me. "You're always wet, aren't you?" He started to thrust inside me, making the side of my head bump into the velvet cushion every few seconds.

My hands slid underneath his shirt to feel his strong abs below the soft skin, to feel his hard pecs above that. My nails started to claw as he pounded into me, and this man made me want to come already. "For you, I am."

He gave a sexy moan and pounded into me harder. "Fuck, baby."

---

We got back the time we lost.

Axel seemed to abandon his work obligations to spend all his time with me. We had breakfast together in the mornings, worked out together in his personal gym, and sometimes we would take a bath together afterward, just soaking in the tub without saying much. We'd make love in the middle of the day and then fall asleep. Instead of eating at home, he would take me out to a restaurant I might enjoy.

There were times when I didn't think about my father at all, because he made it that easy. I suspected that wouldn't be the end of things with my father, and if it wasn't, I was grateful he'd chosen to give me space.

Axel sat across from me at the restaurant, the sleeves of his collared shirt pushed to his elbows, his jawline clean because he'd shaved that morning. He grabbed the wine bottle and refilled his glass before he took a drink. Our silence was spent with his focused stare looking at me like I was the only person in the room.

I was lucky to have a husband look at me like that. A damn fine husband who could have any woman he wanted...but who chose me.

He swirled his glass and took another drink. "You look beautiful tonight."

"Thank you, but you already said that."

"Did I?" he asked, smirking slightly. "Nervous?"

"You always make me a little nervous."

"I meant the restaurant."

"No, I'm excited." It had taken me a long time to realize that it was my dream, that it was where I belonged...not pushing drugs on the street like a criminal. "It's hard to believe I had that other life. I'm ashamed I was ever involved in that lifestyle."

"Ashamed is a strong word."

"It's not my place, and I should have known that sooner."

"But if you had, you wouldn't have met me, and that would be a tragedy."

"Yes, it would be." Every man before Axel felt like a boy. A teenage boy who wouldn't know a real woman if she punched him in the face. "Speaking of which...you've been home a lot. Are you still working with my father?"

He shook his head. "I bowed out."

"You did?"

"I told him he could have it. You're the only thing I wanted anyway."

My heart tightened in warmth. "What about Theo?"

"I tried to get him to bow out too, but he refused. So I guess they're business partners now. To be honest, haven't really talked to either of them about it. It's not my place to be involved anymore."

"I can't pretend I'm not pleased with that answer." I didn't want Axel involved in that world anymore. I didn't want him working with my father. I wanted us to live lives above the table, paying our taxes and obeying the laws...except for public indecency.

"I said when I settled down, I would leave that life."

"You said when you have a family."

"And I do have a family. You're my family, baby." He looked at me with that intense gaze, like I was truly the most wonderful thing that had ever happened to him.

When he said things like that, my body went hot and cold at the same time, and my mouth became parched. "You're my family too, babe."

The waiter brought the food a moment later, serving us our hot dishes. These last few weeks together of drinking and eating had made my clothes feel a little tight, even with the gym sessions. But it was hard not to celebrate like it was our honeymoon.

"A lot of people are coming tomorrow."

"You think?"

"All of our reservations are booked up. Walk-ins will be disappointed."

"People don't show up for reservations all the time."

"Oh, they'll show up for these. According to the papers, this is the hottest restaurant in town."

We'd had food critics come to the restaurant for a special four-course meal prepared for them and a guest. I had been in the kitchen with the rest of the cooking staff, helping them make the dishes for our guests. All of the reviews were glowing—and that definitely fueled interest. "I'm not going to be able to sleep tonight."

"Good," he said after he took a bite. "Because I have other plans anyway."

Dinner started at five in the evening, and since I wasn't working in the kitchen, I got to wear a black cocktail dress and heels, diamonds around my neck and in my lobes. The kitchen staff was ready, the waiters were ready for their tables, and the low lighting with the music had given it the vibe of a club.

Axel was the most dressed up I'd ever seen him except on our wedding day, in slacks that hugged his tight ass nicely and a black collared shirt that fit his chest and shoulders well. His black wedding ring matched his attire. "Here we go, baby."

The doors opened, and fifteen minutes later, people started to show up for their reservations. Alessandra had done a great job preparing the restaurant for its opening weekend because everything seemed to be in place. People were taken to their tables, and the waiters were there to serve them water and present the wine list.

Axel recognized some of the guests, so he greeted them with his charisma and dashing smile. Sometimes, he introduced me to them, saying I was the head chef and the culinary designer for that evening's meal.

Time passed, and soon it was a madhouse, lots of walk-ins that had to be turned away because the reservation list was booked solid—and everyone showed up for dinner.

Axel stared at me, that grin on his face.

"What?"

"Just waiting."

"For...?"

The smile remained, arrogance in his eyes. "For you to admit I was right."

I immediately broke eye contact, afraid he was going to say I told you so.

"That your hole-in-the-wall would have been a mistake."

I looked out the double glass doors to the people mingling outside, wearing their coats because it was still chilly at the beginning of spring.

"Come on." His arm moved around my waist. "Say it." His hand inched to my ass.

I swatted it away. "We're in public."

"Either say it now, or—" he pulled me close and spoke into my ear "—I'll make you say it tonight when we get home, with my dick in your mouth." His big hand grabbed on to my ass.

I pushed his arm away and stepped aside.

He grinned. "I hoped that would be your answer."

More people filed into the restaurant and were led to their tables. Others got comfortable on the velvet couches, the place where Axel had fucked me several times and we'd had to dab the sex spots dry to get rid of the stains. Waiters presented them with flutes of champagne as they waited, and hors d'oeuvres were presented on silver trays.

A line formed next to the hostess stand, and once a couple stepped aside, I saw a familiar face behind them.

My father stood there dressed in slacks and a collared shirt, his assistant at his side in an evening dress. The hostess spoke to him, but his eyes were on me like there was no one else in the room.

I was frozen in place, caught off guard that he had decided to come to my restaurant for dinner. I hadn't expected that, but I should have, because it seemed like exactly something he would do. Unable to recover myself, I only met his look.

Axel approached him but didn't greet him with a handshake. "I hope you have reservations because we have no availability for walk-ins. It's a packed house tonight."

"I made reservations as soon as the system was open." He looked at Axel briefly before his eyes switched back to me. "Congratulations, sweetheart."

I didn't know what to say. I didn't know what to do. So I turned around and headed to the bathroom.

When I came out moments later, Axel was nowhere to be found. He was no longer greeting our guests at the front.

When I looked into the dining area, I found his muscular back facing me. He sat at a table across from my father, the two of them locked in deep conversation under the mood lighting. My father's assistant looked at her phone like the conversation didn't concern her.

I was annoyed my father was there. But I was more annoyed that Axel had chosen to sit with him rather than stand with me. I looked out the double doors and did my best to pretend I didn't feel betrayed. Greeting people and forming connections out of thin air wasn't my strongest suit. With me, it would just look awkward and forced, so I chose to stand there and stay quiet.

Moments later, Axel came back to my side. "It looks like your father and his assistant are an item."

I ignored him.

"Baby?"

"We're having our grand opening right now. Why are you talking to him?"

His playful eyes suddenly hardened. "Just saying hello."

"Hello to the man who threatened to kill you?"

"Baby, he's your father."

"He's an asshole for showing up here on my big night. Instead of letting me have this moment, he had to make it about himself."

"I think he just wanted to support you."

"He could have supported me when I asked for a loan—but he hesitated." I looked out the window again.

His arm moved around my waist. "Baby, it's okay."

"We've had such a nice night together...and then he ruins it."

"He didn't ruin it. He just wanted to have dinner and support you." He moved in front of me, blocking my view of the window and the guests who were waiting for their tables. "Forget about it, alright? It's done. He's over there having dinner with what's-her-name, and you're here with me."

"You weren't here with me when you walked over there."

His eyes flicked back and forth between mine. "I just wanted to say hello. It's called manners."

"You owe him nothing, and you know it."

"He's my father-in-law. While I don't hold him in the highest regard, he's your family, and he's still important to you, whether you admit it or not. I don't want you to have this hate in your heart. It's the same hate my parents carry —and it's aged them decades. The past is gone. It's been resolved. Try to let it go."

# Chapter 17

## *Axel*

Scarlett was angry with me.

I could tell because she wouldn't make eye contact with me. When she got to our bedroom, she dropped her clothes and immediately washed her face, as if removing her makeup would somehow deter my desire.

It was two in the morning, and our grand opening had been a success. But now, there was a sourness between us that turned the air rancid. I hadn't mentioned her father for weeks on purpose because I wanted to savor this honeymoon phase, but I'd known it would only last so long before reality hit us in the face again.

She got into bed and turned on her side, dismissing me.

I did my nighttime routine then got into bed beside her. I lay there and stared at the dark ceiling. I could tell she was wide awake because of the way she breathed. She wasn't even tired, based on how labored her breaths sounded. "Baby."

She lay still and silent.

"The last thing I want is for this to come between us. I'm sure you agree."

She lay there.

"Baby, come on."

She continued to ignore me.

"Don't make me come over there."

She pulled the sheet farther up her shoulder.

I slid across the bed and came up behind her, my big body pressed up against her littler one. My arm circled over her tummy, and I pulled her close, letting her boil in my heat, letting her feel my hard muscles. I took a breath and let her feel my chest rise and move her with it. "I'm sorry that you're upset. But don't be upset with me."

After a long stretch of silence, she finally caved. "I know you have good intentions."

"I always have good intentions with you."

We sat together at the dining table, having dinner with the laptop open, looking over the numbers for the first weekend at the restaurant.

She had been so good at bookkeeping for her father that managing the expenses of a restaurant was a walk in the park for her. She had everything organized into Excel spreadsheets and even had analysis reports. She did them on a daily basis, and I thought that was overkill.

I pulled the laptop toward me and looked through it. "It's hard to get the full financial picture in just a weekend, but it looks like things are good."

"Things will slow down after the grand opening."

"Maybe they won't."

"That's just how it is."

"You're awfully pessimistic, even after a grand-slam opening."

"I'm just trying to be realistic." She pulled the computer back and closed the lid.

Aldo knocked on my bedroom door. We'd just received our dinner not too long ago, so the plates were nowhere near ready to be collected. He'd hardly given us half an hour. He poked his head inside. "Your father is here to see you."

I turned to Scarlett, knowing this would drain the blood out of her face. She'd just gotten back to being in a good mood, but now that would be shattered into hundreds of pieces.

"I don't want to see him," she said quietly, looking down at her plate.

"I'm sorry, I was unclear." Aldo looked at me. "I'm referring to *your* father, sir."

All of Scarlett's anger dissolved. Her gaze immediately lifted to me, her eyes wide in surprise.

I continued to stare at Aldo, and I felt my heart stop. Seconds passed, and then I looked at Scarlett, but it was one of the few times when I didn't actually see her face. It was just a haze. "Did he say what he wants?"

"No, sir."

"Are you sure it's him?"

"Absolutely, sir," he said. "It's been a while since I've seen him, but I would never forget his face."

Adrenaline. Dread. Terror. I felt no excitement or joy. I was actually a little scared. Not scared that he would hurt me physically, but that he would somehow hurt me more emotionally...if that was even possible at this point. "I'll be right there."

When I entered the parlor, I found my father standing in front of the fire, one hand in his pocket, his eyes on the flames inside the hearth like he was mesmerized by their movements. He was still, his back slightly bent because his posture had stooped in recent years. His old watch was still on his right wrist.

I stood there and took him in, my mind unable to believe the truth that my eyes screamed. He was really there, in the flesh, and he didn't seem to have paperwork for me to sign or a lawyer to bear witness.

If he'd come all the way here and stepped into my house, he must have something important to say. "Hey, Dad."

The sound of my voice made him whip his head around from the fireplace and look at me. His blue eyes widened in surprise at my appearance, but then they slowly turned guarded with discomfort, like being in the room with me was inherently awkward.

I moved to the armchair and took a seat, while he continued to stand. My elbow propped on the armrest, and my fingertips rested against my lips. My eyes took in the sight of him by the fireplace, but it was still hard to grapple with reality. It was really him, not a ghost. "Take a seat."

He looked at the armchair across from me and, after a moment of silent deliberation, sat down. He looked at me across the table, eyes on mine for the first time. Normally, he avoided my stare, focused on paperwork in front of him or hiding behind sunglasses. But now, he actually looked at me.

I was desperate for a cigar, something to coat my tongue to make this tension more tolerable, but I would never light up in front of my father, someone who didn't smoke. A decanter of scotch was sitting there, but I didn't pour a glass or offer him one.

The silence continued, the crackling from the fireplace the only sound in the quiet room.

He was the one who'd come to me, so I decided to let him speak first—in case I shoved my foot in my mouth.

He gave a sigh, the same sigh I remembered from my childhood, and brought his hands together in his lap. "The man who shot me in the arm...he came by the house. Told your mother and me that he'd threatened to kill us both if you didn't stay away from his daughter...the woman you are now married to. You ended things with her to keep us alive, even though you were in love with her. We disowned you... but you continued to protect us."

I felt my breath give me away. I sucked in a deep breath I didn't know I needed until it happened.

"He took responsibility for everything and asked that we not blame you for his actions. His daughter no longer speaks to him because of the things he's done...and he doesn't want that to happen to us."

I had no idea what Dante could have possibly said to make my father listen, not after shooting him in the arm, but he somehow pulled a rabbit out of a hat like the best showman.

"He also said you're innocent of the crimes you were accused of...and showed us proof."

"What proof?" I blurted.

"Surveillance footage of her infidelity before the marriage ended, bank statements detailing her erratic spending, emails to your lawyer about getting the prenup changed and forging your signature. He pieced everything together and wove a story, that my son gave his heart to the wrong woman and she burned him to the ground. What's more... he said you left your previous career to settle down."

All I could do was sit there with a hard stare, unable to believe that my father had just said all that. It'd been a long time since we'd had a conversation like this—years ago, before I went to prison. After I was incarcerated, we didn't speak for two years because they never came to visit.

My father stared at the coffee table for a while. "I want to apologize...but I'm not sure it'll do much good."

"I don't want an apology."

He looked up to meet my stare, guarded once more.

"I just want my dad." I felt no resentment toward him or Mom. They'd turned their backs on me when they should have been by my side through the entire ordeal, but I didn't care. I didn't care about all the horrible things they'd said to me. My father was there, sitting across from me, and not looking at me with shame. I was grateful that this reunion had happened at all, that my dad hadn't collapsed from a heart attack and I'd had to live with that regret. He was there with me. We had a second chance.

My dad closed his eyes briefly, like that somehow made him feel worse. "Alexander..." He didn't say anything else, as if saying more than just my name would be too much.

I left my chair and came around the coffee table. His eyes were still downcast as I reached my hand out for him to grab. "Get your ass up and hug me, old man."

A slight smirk spread over his mouth before he looked up at me. "How can you just let this go? After everything that's happened. After everything we said and did. How can it be this easy?"

I kept my hand there. "I held a grudge against someone I loved before, and I won't make that mistake again."

His stare washed over my face before he took my hand and let me pull him up. He was a few inches shorter than me, life compressing his spine, but his features still reminded me of my own. He grabbed me by the shoulder and looked me over, just the way he used to when I'd finished a game or completed a performance with the orchestra. Pride swept through him before he pulled me in for an embrace, a squeeze he hadn't given me in so long I'd forgotten how it felt to be hugged by my own father.

Peace like I'd never known swept through me. The stress of the estrangement, of their disappointment, all the rage I'd felt toward the woman who'd locked me up and thrown away the key...it all disappeared.

"I love you, son."

My breath caught in my throat, and my eyes closed. He used to say it every time we got off the phone, said it so often that it sounded automatic. But once I was put on trial, he'd never said it again—not in person, not over the phone. He said it now, and it sounded just the way it used to. "I love you, Dad."

When I walked in the bedroom door, Scarlett was standing there like she'd been pacing since I left. The remains of our dinner were untouched, and so was the wine. She whipped toward me, her eyes scanning my expression for news.

"What happened?" she asked.

"He apologized. I forgave him."

"Really? What—what brought this on? This is so random… just came out of nowhere. No one is sick, right?"

"No one is sick," I said quickly. "But it didn't come out of nowhere."

"Then where did it come from?" she asked quietly.

It was the last answer I'd ever expected to give. "Your father."

"My—my father?" She stepped back as if the words made her stumble. "What does he have to do with this?"

I explained everything her father had done, how he'd told my father I'd lost my girl to protect him, that I was truly innocent in that legal debacle. "He must have used a lot of resources to pull together all the information, called in some favors to get those phone records and surveillance footage. He basically built my case better than my own lawyers did."

She was stunned into silence.

"And your father told my dad that he knows what it's like to be estranged from your child...and he didn't want that for us."

Her arms tightened over her chest, and she looked determined to shut out the information, to not feel anything for her father's actions. She looked elsewhere, breathing harder than normal, trying to sort it out in her pretty little head.

"He righted his wrongs," I said. "That's what he did."

Her eyes found mine. "I'm happy for you. There are no words to describe just how happy I am that this has happened for you."

"I know."

She moved into my chest and squeezed me.

My chin dropped onto her head, and I squeezed her back tightly, my life complete for the first time.

She stayed there for a long while, letting me hold her as she held me.

I could do this forever, live in the moment with her, a very good moment. "We're going to dinner with them tomorrow."

"We?" she asked as she pulled away to see my face.

"Damn right, we," I said. "I want them to meet my wife."

"I just thought you'd want time with them alone first."

"You're my family. Where I go, you go."

Her eyes melted like hot butter.

"And you know where we're going?" I grinned, knowing she would guess it.

Her eyes flicked back and forth between mine as the smile moved into her features. "Seriously?"

"It's my favorite place. And I want my parents to see it."

"I don't want to come across like I'm showing off..."

"I know what my parents like, and they'll love your food," I said. "And they'll *love* you."

"I don't know... I was pretty rude to them."

"You weren't rude. You stood up for me. Big difference."

"I hope they'll see it that way," she said. "First impressions are lasting impressions."

I wasn't the least bit worried about it. Scarlett had a smile that lit up the room, showed affection in just her words, without needing touch. She was endearing and funny. She was a hot piece of ass with the full package. "I'm not worried about it. And if it makes you feel better, they could dislike you all they want, and it's not going to change anything."

I could tell that meant a lot to her by the way her eyes softened, the way she looked up at me like I was the best gift that had ever appeared under her Christmas tree. Her hand went to my arm, and she touched me, gently felt the muscles under my skin. "I love you."

I would never grow tired of hearing that. "I know." I pulled her in close and pressed a kiss to her lips, but the second I felt her mouth, all that affection transformed into something more. A spark lit the match, and then the flames erupted around us on all sides. It happened anytime I touched her, but it really exploded now.

My hand slid into her hair, and I kissed her as I backed her up into the couch. I slid the other underneath her top and grabbed her tit, squeezing it hard underneath her bra and making her wince slightly. She was taller than most women, which I loved, but she was still so petite, so small in my big grasp.

Her hands dove underneath my shirt, and her nails started to dig their grooves into my flesh, her head tilted back to accept my anxious kiss. Our mouths danced in fire, and once the steam started to billow, she yanked my shirt over my head. A satisfied moan left her lips when she saw my bare chest, her favorite part of my physique besides my arms...and my dick.

Our embrace became too intimate for the couch, so I lifted her into my arms and carried her like she weighed nothing, because in comparison to the tractor tires I pushed around in my gym, she really did weigh nothing.

I dropped her on the bed and yanked off my jeans and shoes, so anxious for her, it was like I'd never fucked her before. In these heated moments, it always felt that way, our hundredth time feeling like our first time.

Too anxious to wait for me to undress her, she kicked away her bottoms and left her top in place.

My knees hit the mattress, and I moved on top of her, yanking her shirt and bra up to expose her tits. With her soft thighs on either side of my hips, she took my length, took it with a loud groan like she'd somehow forgotten what my dick could do.

Fully sheathed inside my wife, I held myself as I looked at her, her lips hungry for my kiss, desperate for it. Ever since the first moment I saw her, I wanted her. I wanted her in every dirty way I could imagine. Lots of nasty shit had crossed my mind when I saw her sitting there across the dining room from me, her legs crossed in her flirty dress in the spring heat. While that desire still burned white-hot, it had grown into something more, something deeper. It made me slow down, made me rock into her at a steady pace rather than a sprint, made me kiss her throughout, made me whisper my love against her ear. It made me want to love rather than fuck—because I was madly in love with her.

# Chapter 18

## *Scarlett*

We walked up to the restaurant, my restaurant, and Axel opened the door for me to walk inside. At a quick glance, everything seemed to be functioning the way it was supposed to. The music played over the speakers, and guests enjoyed champagne and appetizers in the lounge like they were about to attend a cocktail party. The tables were full, the waiters were ready, and the atmosphere was exactly what Axel and I had imagined.

Axel spoke to Alessandra at the front. "My parents are probably already here. They're old, so fifteen minutes early is right on time for them."

She chuckled then guided us to the table.

I was nervous, so nervous it felt like a frog was in my throat. The second I tried to talk, I'd probably croak, and they'd look at me with disgust. When Axel told me their opinion didn't matter to him, I believed him. But their opinion still mattered to me.

Axel took my hand and guided me to the table.

I saw them from a distance away, sitting side by side, looking exactly as I remembered but a little less timid.

"You guys are still early to everything, huh?" Axel said as his dad stood up to greet him.

"And you're still late," he said with a chuckle.

The two men embraced in a tight hug.

It was hard not to smile.

His mother got up next, moving into his chest and squeezing him tightly, a foot shorter than him and petite like me.

It was hard to imagine she'd given birth to that man.

They spoke to each other quietly for a few moments, their meeting clearly emotional.

His father turned to me. "We haven't properly met. Henry." He extended his hand to shake mine.

I took it. "It's lovely to meet you. Properly." I cleared my throat, remembering our last interaction perfectly. "I know our first meeting was a bit tense. I just want you to know I'm not really the confrontational type—"

"It's okay," he said. "My wife and I deserved it. Water under the bridge."

"Yes...water under the bridge."

"My job was to have Axel learn from me, but I'm the one who should be taking a page from his book."

I smiled. "He's very wise."

When Axel broke apart from his mother, he introduced me. "Mom, this is Scarlett, my very sexy wife."

"Oh my god." I stood there in embarrassment, unable to believe he'd said that.

But both of his parents chuckled.

"It's lovely to meet you." I shook her hand. "I'm excited we're all here together this evening."

"Me too," his mother said. "Me too."

---

"That went well." Axel loosened his watch and walked into the closet to put it away.

"Yeah, it did." I sat at the foot of the bed and slipped off my heels.

He came back out of the closet, his shirt gone and the belt from his slacks missing. "I can tell they liked you."

"They just met me."

"But I can tell. What did you think of them?"

"Well..." I stood up and unzipped the back of my dress so I could step out of it. "I guess it's more difficult for me to forget the way they treated you. I remember watching you go through their rejection. I find this a little harder to accept."

He regarded me for a moment, his blue eyes having beautiful depth. "I think if you love someone enough, it's easy to accept them without reservations. Even in our estrangement and silence, I still loved them. I wouldn't have protected them otherwise."

"I know."

"So I guess it's easy for me to forgive and forget. Theo taught me that."

"Theo?" I asked incredulously. "He doesn't strike me as the forgive-and-forget type."

"Well, that's not the lesson he was trying to impart, but it's the lesson that came across."

"When did this happen?"

He moved to the armchair and took a seat, the top of his slacks fastened with his dress shoes still on. Both elbows moved to the armrests. "When I was angry and ended things with you, I told Theo I was done. Ready to move on. But then he asked if he could take you out. I thought it was a bluff at first. Theo is a really good liar, so it's hard to know with him. But he continued on and said if I was done with you, why couldn't he have you since you two...had chemistry...as he put it. That was all it took for me to pull my head out of my ass. Because the idea of you with him, or anyone else, made me sick. That was when I realized I didn't care what your shortcomings were. I love you, and that's all that matters. So I came back...and you were nice enough not to make me beg."

"I wanted you so much, I would have begged."

He smirked slightly. "Anyway, that's when I learned that lesson. And I think it's something you should take to heart."

My heart folded over in my chest because I knew what direction he was about to take this in. "It's not the same thing—"

"If he died tomorrow, would you be devastated?"

"Just because I don't want a relationship doesn't mean I want him dead."

"Not the same thing," he said. "Now, answer the question."

"No." I took a seat on the foot of the bed again.

He continued to watch me. "Baby—"

"Don't tell me what to do or how I should feel."

"I did neither of those things. I asked you *how* you felt, and you won't answer because it's not the answer you want to give."

"With all the shit he did—"

"He made it right with my parents. He exonerated me of a crime I didn't commit—which had nothing to do with him. When I begged him for you, he did try to steer you back toward me. It doesn't excuse what he did, but it shows that he does care. He just has an odd way of showing it sometimes."

My arms tightened and I looked away.

"I know how much you care about him. I know this pain is eating at your heart every day. That's how you die at thirty-five from a heart attack. Stress. It's the silent killer."

I continued to avoid his stare.

"I support whatever you decide. But I think if we were to give your father another chance, it would be different this time."

"We just had a nice dinner. Let's forget about this."

"Well, I can't just forget about it," he said. "Because as far as I'm concerned, your father and I have buried the hatchet. I need to pay him a visit and thank him for what he did. I'd appreciate it if you came with me."

I rose off the bed and walked into the closet, letting my dress fall to the floor. One of his t-shirts was folded in the drawer, so I pulled it over my head and wore it like a blanket with sleeves. It was time for bed and I was tired, but my heart raced like I was about to head out for a run.

Axel came into the closet and leaned against the door-frame. With his arms crossed over his chest, he watched me. "I know you must feel some gratitude toward him. I know you must admire what he did, what I couldn't even do."

"Can we just go to bed—"

"All I've ever wanted is you. And I know you two come as a set. You belong as a set."

"Axel—"

"Just come with me. You don't have to say anything if you don't want to." He blocked the doorway with his massive size, telling me that this conversation wouldn't end until I agreed to his terms.

"Fine. I'll come with you."

---

We pulled up onto the property and parked the car. I looked at the three-story villa, the place where I'd grown up, the place to which I'd thought I would never return. My heart had the pace of a hummingbird's wings, fluttering in my chest in terror. I was nervous to see him, although I wasn't sure why.

I was right. He was wrong.

Axel opened the door then came around to get me. My door was open, but I remained in my seat, my safety belt still strapped across my chest. In early spring, it was still dark earlier than I preferred, so winter's bite maintained its grip.

Axel continued to stare at me. "You don't have to talk." He leaned down and hit the button with his finger, making the strap come free from my shoulder. "Come on." He gave me his hand.

I released a sigh before I took it, feeling his strong arm pull me up to my feet.

"Attagirl." His arm moved around me as he escorted me to the front double doors. We let ourselves inside since he was expecting us, and once we entered the parlor, we saw my father sitting on the couch, waiting for us. Normally, he let his butler handle his guests and came out at his leisure, but now he was the one who was anxious to see us.

He didn't seem to have expected me to come because his eyes widened slightly at the sight of me. A fire burned in the black marble fireplace. Everything was dark and chic, with pendant lighting in places, dark couches, a place that clearly belonged to a bachelor but still had the touch of a woman.

He rose to his feet, eyes still on me, forgetting Axel entirely.

Axel brought me close then moved in front of me to take my father's hand. "Thanks for seeing me, Dante."

His eyes were still on me. "The pleasure is mine, Axel."

Axel moved to the couch.

I stood there and met my father's stare.

He looked at me with a mixture of fear and joy, like he was happy I was there but also terrified of what I might say. "I'm happy to see you, sweetheart."

My eyes moved down, and I took the seat beside Axel.

My father watched me then released a quiet breath in disappointment. He turned to his place across from Axel. The coffee table was laden with bottles of wine and glasses, along with marinated olives, olive oil, and feta cubes. Fresh bread had been set out as well.

My father took the heat off me and looked at Axel instead. "How can I help you?"

"My father told me what you did." Axel cut right to the chase, got straight to the point, didn't waste my time or my father's. There was no other reason for Axel to be there because they were no longer business partners. Now their only connection was familial, as crazy as that sounded. "Not only did you tell him I lost the love of my life to keep him alive because I was pinned under your thumb, but you proved my innocence."

My father's eyes dropped like he didn't want the praise.

"If you hadn't proved my innocence, telling him you were responsible for the bullet in his arm wouldn't have mattered. How did you do that?"

He stared at the floor for a while before he lifted his gaze to meet Axel's. "I hired a lot of people. A lot of PIs. Leveraged my connections in law enforcement. Spoke to the tech nerds I know to pull all the feeds I needed, breaking government protocol. I've made a lot of useful contacts in my long career."

"That must have taken an entire team."

"A team of thirty people, yeah," he said. "But I'm glad I did it because you were telling the truth all along."

"I'd like to pay you for those expenses—"

"You owe me nothing."

"That must have cost you millions."

"Consider it a payment for all your pain and suffering." He glanced at me and then looked at Axel again. "I hope the revelation allowed you to reconnect with your parents."

"It did," Axel said. "We had dinner together the other night. All four of us."

My father gave a nod. "I imagine they loved my daughter."

"How could they not?" Axel smiled slightly. "Thank you for what you did."

"Don't thank me," he said simply. "It was the least I could do in light of all the hardship I caused you."

Axel bowed his head and rubbed his palms together, thinking of his next words. "I spoke to Theo about the business. I was unable to persuade him to return the whole business to you. I'm sorry, but I can't control what he does."

"It doesn't matter," he said. "I've decided to retire."

I felt the flush of surprise rush through me like an electrical shock. My dad always said he would only retire when he dropped dead. But now, he seemed to do it willingly.

"Really?" Axel asked in mild surprise.

"Yes." He rested his ankle on the opposite knee, his elbow propped on the armrest. "Theo is the sole owner of that business now. I wish him the best."

"Why?" Axel asked.

He was quiet for a long time before he sucked in a slow breath and released it. "There's more to life than power. Than money. I should focus my time on things that are important, like family...relationships...peace. Going to a nice restaurant and enjoying myself. Finding a woman to be my wife and partner. To prioritize the things that matter. Up until this point, I've only prioritized the things that don't matter...to my detriment and utter ruin. Won't make the same mistake twice."

I looked at the coffee table, unable to believe he'd said all of that.

Axel turned to look at me, his eyes silently asking if I had anything to say.

My hands bunched together in my lap, and my eyes flicked down again.

Axel continued to stare, pressuring me with his intensity. When I said nothing, he left the couch and stepped away. "I'll let you guys talk." He headed to the front door.

"You said I didn't have to talk."

He looked at me over his shoulder before he proceeded to the front door. "Then don't talk." He walked out and stepped into the darkness, content being in the cold because he ran hot like the desert.

I looked at my father.

His stare was on me.

I didn't know what to say, so I sat there in silence.

"I would apologize again, but I don't think another apology is what you need to hear."

I wasn't sure what I needed to hear to make this right.

"I miss you."

I turned my head and looked at the other wall.

"You're my best friend. I realize that now that I don't have you."

I continued to give him the cold shoulder.

"I love the restaurant. It's far more beautiful and grander than I expected...and I already expected so much. And the food... I definitely ate my carbs that night."

He tried to pull at my heartstrings, but I refused to let him.

"You're still angry with me."

"Did you expect me to forget everything in a couple weeks?" I turned to look at him head on.

"No," he said calmly. "But I hoped you would realize how sorry I am. You would realize that I've changed—for good. I've made amends with your husband, not just for you, but because I've grown to respect him. If I could choose any man in the world for you, I would choose him."

My arms crossed over my chest because a draft had filled the room after Axel stepped out. It took a minute for it to reach me, but when it did, the bumps formed.

"You're my entire life," he said, his eyes filling with emotion, his voice matching it. "And now that I don't have you...it hurts every day. I should have let Axel take the business and opened that restaurant with you. I should have taken you on a trip to Paris so we could visit all the bakeries you like. Instead of breaking necks and doing backdoor deals, I should have spent my time with you. I should have shielded you from this life rather than tried to groom you for it. If you can never forgive me for what I've done, I understand that. But could you please accept this is who I am now...and give me another chance."

"I—I feel like I don't know you. Everything we had before was a lie. How can I trust anything you say?"

His eyes flinched in pain before he retreated and looked away.

"Lies after lies...after lies."

"That's not who I am anymore—"

"Then I'm meeting you for the first time," I snapped. "I've never really known you."

"I may have lied about things to manipulate events, but I've never lied about my love for you. All of that was real. You know that."

I looked down at my hands again.

"Sweetheart...please."

"I'm glad Axel has started a new relationship with his parents. I'm grateful that you gave that to him, and I appreciate everything it took to make it happen. But I'm not sure if that's right for us."

My father inhaled a deep and painful breath, the kind that nearly made him choke, like he sucked on his cigar too hard and directed the smoke into his sinuses instead of his mouth. A sheen moved over the surface of his eyes, and instead of being the strong man he always displayed, he succumbed to quiet tears.

He bowed his head, doing the best he could to hide them.

It killed me to see him like this. It hurt so much that I couldn't tolerate it anymore. I left the couch and moved around the opposite way, avoiding his stare as much as possible until my back was to him. Then I walked out the double doors and joined Axel on the wet pavement.

He looked at me, and with just a single glance, he figured out what had happened. "I hope you change your mind."

---

I lay in bed beside him, waiting for him to speak his thoughts on what had happened with my father. It'd been a quiet drive home, the air heavy with tension, and when we got into the bedroom, it became worse.

Now we were in bed, lights off, lying together in the dark.

"Are you mad at me?" I whispered, looking at the ceiling.

"No. Why would I be?"

"Because I didn't bury the hatchet with my father."

"Just because I disagree with it doesn't mean I don't support you. If you aren't ready, you aren't ready. Simple as that."

He let me off the hook, but somehow, I didn't feel better.

"But I admit I thought you would be touched by the things he said."

"Such as?"

"Retirement. Prioritizing the things that matter. You basically have your father back, the version of him that you deserved in the first place. Keeping your distance and hiding behind your grudge seems like a waste."

"Even if it is, I'm just not there. I can't move past his betrayals so easily."

"I never said it was easy."

"Well, you sure make it look it."

We lay there in silence for a while. It was one of the rare times when we didn't have sex before we went to sleep. There was too much heaviness in the air for that. My thoughts were on other things, not my husband.

"Time heals all wounds," he said. "Perhaps you just need more of it."

"Maybe..."

He moved to me, scooping me into his arms and spooning me from behind, hugging me the way a grizzly bear would hug a cub. His face moved into my hair then he lay still, ready for sleep.

I lay awake for a while longer until I fell asleep.

---

I was jarred awake by something. Just wasn't sure what.

Axel had jerked upright in bed, his breathing escalated.

I thought I'd heard a gunshot, but maybe I'd just heard him. "What—what was that?"

He jumped out of his bed and snatched his phone off his nightstand. He never answered me.

Something felt wrong...very wrong, so I sat up in bed and stared at him.

He opened his phone, and the light lit up his face in the dark. His thumb scrolled then he opened an app. He seemed to be looking at his security system. He started to flick through the camera feed, looking from one image to the next.

My heart started to race. The sweat came from nowhere and formed on my forehead instantly. "Axel?"

"Fuck." He headed to the closet.

"What's happening?" I got out of bed, and my leg got caught on the sheet, making me trip to the floor.

Axel didn't check if I was okay, which told me this was bad.

He came out of the closet and flicked on the lights. He put on his black sweatpants, a bulletproof vest over his bare chest, and in his arms was a heavy black gun, a *big* one, like the kind the military carried. I didn't know anything about guns, but it looked like one of those automatic ones that fired a ton of bullets at once.

"Okay...what the fuck is going on?"

At that moment, the alarm must have been tripped, given the sirens coming from the hallway.

I was in nothing but his t-shirt, standing there utterly useless as someone invaded our home. I hoped it was a dumb burglar who'd just picked the wrong house, but my heart told me it wasn't.

"Get dressed." He barked his order without looking at me, typing on his phone like he was sending a text.

I didn't ask questions and did as he asked. I put on whatever I could find, my dark-blue pajamas bottoms and flip-flops. My hair was in disarray, and I quickly put it up in a bun so it wouldn't get in my way.

"Take this." He handed me a handgun and a vest that fit me like a dress. "You know how to use it, right?" He was serious but spoke calmly, while I was about to hyperventilate.

I took the cold metal and gave a nod.

"The safety is off."

"Okay." I pointed the gun to the floor. "What's happening?"

"They're in the house."

"Who's they?"

"I don't know," he snapped. "Security is dead. Aldo is in the safe room."

"Uh, we have a safe room...?"

"We don't have time now. Whoever is here, they know what they're doing. Aldo dispatched more men. They're on their way."

It was hard to form words, not when I could barely breathe. "How long will it take?"

He walked into the other room and ignored what I said.

"Axel, what are we going to do?"

"These doors are bulletproof." I'd thought the space was open between the living quarters and the bedroom, but now I could see there were doors hidden in the walls. He pushed his palm into the molding, and the doors popped out so they could slide closed. "Shut the doors and lock yourself on the inside."

"What—what about you?"

"I'll kill them."

"By—by yourself?"

"Baby, we don't have time for this. We probably have seconds. Shut this door and lock it." He was red in the face. "Do you understand me? Don't open this door for anything, no matter what you hear. I can hold them off until help comes, but I can't do it if I'm worried about you."

"Oh Jesus..." I started to cry, holding the little gun to my side.

"Baby, look at me."

I started to sob, scared what would happen on the other side of the door.

"Hey." He grabbed my shoulder and shook it. "Focus. Now."

"I can't lose you—"

"You won't. Now get your ass in there and lock the door—"

"Axel."

"*Don't make me ask you again!*" He shoved me across the floor and rolled the heavy doors shut.

It had a big lock in the center, something that kept the doors in place. I turned the knob and heard the unmistakable click. I gulped down a couple heavy breaths before I ran to my phone on the nightstand. Without thinking, I grabbed it and called the first person who came to mind.

My father.

As if he'd been waiting for my call, he answered before the first ring finished. "Sweetheart—"

"Dad, I need help." Tears crackled in my voice, and I gave a jolt when I heard distant shouting. I wasn't sure if Axel was still in the living room, or if he'd left through the door of the suite and ran into the hallway. The alarm continued to blare.

"What's happening?" he blurted, his gentle voice now authoritative.

"I—I don't know." I said everything as fast as I could. "Men are in the house...guards are dead...alarm is going off."

"I'm sending my men now. Hold tight."

"Wait, don't go."

"I'll call you right back." *Click.*

I sat on the rug on the floor, the gun held in my hand, leaning against the side of the bed as I continued to hyperventilate. It was Axel against who knew how many men, and I was there alone, unable to help.

The phone rang.

My finger was so sweaty, it slid across the screen in my desperation to answer it. "Dad?"

"I deployed my guys." I heard the sound of walking. Doors slamming. "I'm on my way."

"You're coming?"

"Of course, sweetheart." He pulled the phone away and spoke to the driver. "Get around them. Come on." He came back to the phone. "Where are you in the house?"

"In the bedroom. Axel closed a wall, said it's bulletproof."

"Good. Do you have a weapon?"

"A pistol."

"Do you see anything bigger?"

"I—I don't know. This is what he handed me."

"Sweetheart, you need to be quiet and just wait."

"Axel is out there by himself..."

My father didn't have anything to say to that.

"He should have hidden in here with me."

"If he did that, he would be leading them right to you. If he's what they want, they'll take him and leave you be."

Tears rolled down my cheeks.

"It's exactly what I would have wanted him to do."

I sat there and breathed into the phone, alternating between sobs and quiet cries, and then painful silence.

My dad stayed on the phone with me. "You're going to be alright, sweetheart."

"I'm not worried about me. I'm worried about him."

# Chapter 19

## *Axel*

I stopped by my study and popped my earbuds into my ear. I called Aldo, and he answered right away.

"Sir, are you alright?"

"Are the cameras working?" The safe room had access to hidden cameras positioned throughout the house. The visibility was poor, because the cameras were inside statues and paintings, not always at eye level, to make their presence less obvious.

"The regular security cameras have been destroyed. They shot at them as soon as they came in."

"And the others?" I opened one of the drawers and pulled out a knife before I dropped it into my pocket.

"They remain intact." His voice was audible because the safe room was soundproof. The obnoxious alarm was no longer blaring. "Most of them are on the second floor, but they're coming to the third."

"Can you turn off the alarm?"

"I assumed you wanted it on."

"It's not like the police are coming. My guys are on the way. What's outside?"

"They have a couple armored trucks. They're prepared for visitors."

"Can you figure out who's in charge?"

"No," Aldo answered. "They all look like soldiers."

"So whoever this is doesn't do his own dirty work."

"Looks like that way."

"Aldo, I need you to guide me. I've got to clear out these assholes and keep them away from Scarlett."

"I'll do the best I can," he said. "They reached the top of the stairs. Half are turning left. Half are turning right."

"How many?"

"Three on the left. Two on the right."

I moved to the door and stood against the wall. "I'm in the study."

"Yes, I can see you. They're heavily armored, so I don't think that rifle will do much."

"Thanks for the tip." I put down the rifle and pulled out the knife.

"One of them is about to enter the study."

The knob turned quietly and then he flung the door open, giving a sweep of the room with his rifle. When he spotted me, there was an instant of recognition, but I pushed his barrel to the ceiling and twisted the gun before he could pull the trigger. The knife went straight into his neck, and he stumbled forward.

I caught him, getting blood all over me, but I stopped his body from making a loud thud against the hardwood floor.

"One of them is approaching the bedroom. The other is in the guest bedroom."

I moved into the hallway and snuck up on him from behind. My arm circled his neck, and I stabbed the knife through the plates of his armor before he could release a scream. I caught his body and steadied it before it fell, but I didn't have time to hide his corpse because the other one was coming out of the guest room.

There were ten feet between us, so a stealth attack wouldn't work.

He raised his gun and pointed it at me.

Bullets sprayed the wall as I dodged away. The sound of firing bullets echoed in the hallway, and I knew Scarlett could hear that loud and clear. I got behind a pillar just in time, and the stone took the brunt of the damage, while I slipped into a guest bedroom. Underneath the bed, a rifle was strapped in place. I grabbed it just before the guy walked in with his muzzle pointed at me.

I fired first, spraying him with bullets until he stumbled sideways from the momentum. But he was still alive because he fired his gun at me underneath the bed.

I jumped over the mattress and landed on top of him, knocking the gun away before he could squeeze the trigger again. My fist hit the front of his helmet and shattered it before I shoved the knife right through his neck.

He went still, choking for seconds, and then died.

I moved back into the hallway, seeing the rest of the men coming for me.

I had to get off this floor and lead them away from Scarlett.

They opened fire, and I ducked back into the office, the bullets marking the walls and destroying the paintings and the moldings. I poked my head out and fired back, knowing I had to get a lot of bullets in to defeat the carbon fiber armor they wore from head to toe. They weren't regular henchmen that I'd encountered, who came in armed with just a gun and a bulletproof vest. These guys were practically SWAT.

Who the fuck wanted me dead?

Back and forth, bullets were exchanged. Some of them started to fall.

"More of them are coming from the bottom floor," Aldo said.

"How many?"

"At least a dozen."

"Goddammit." I stepped out again and sprayed them with bullets, taking them down because they hadn't expected me to lunge right toward them like that. After they all collapsed, I grabbed a fresh gun because I was out of ammo and headed to the stairs. I took them two at a time as I headed down, and when I reached the railing that stretched along the second floor, I put the strap of the gun around me, climbed over, and then swung myself forward and dropped down to the first floor. I landed behind the twelve guys, and I quickly scrambled to my feet to raise my gun.

They turned at the sound, but the stairs were precarious as they pivoted, so their response wasn't as fast as it would normally be.

I fired the rifle and knocked half of them down, shells littering the floor around me. The destruction was enough of a distraction for me to run and head down the stairs to the ground level.

"Axel, there are even more by the entryway."

"Fuck."

I could head out the back and run, but if I did that, Scarlett would be here alone. They may not realize she was even there. They might chase me instead. But what if they didn't?

"Axel, someone else is here."

"Is it my guys?"

"No, someone else. They overrode the security system and closed the gates."

"Who the fuck is it?"

"He just got out of the car. He's tall. Wearing all black. No armor."

Definitely the boss.

"He's coming inside," he said. "What are you going to do?"

The men from upstairs were running down to get me, and the boss was about to step inside and finish me off. My guys couldn't get to me with the gate closed, at least not for a while. But all I cared about was Scarlett. "Fuck."

"I don't know what to do."

"Aldo, I need you to do something for me."

"Anything, sir."

"I'm going to hand myself over. I need you to get Scarlett and bring her into the safe room. Ignore whatever happens to me."

Aldo was silent.

"Can you do that for me?"

"I'll call her and guide her down. Is that okay?"

"Yes, that should work."

"Thank you."

"Of course, sir. I'm—I'm so sorry."

"It's fine," I said. "Tell her I love her, alright?"

He hesitated before he answered. "I will."

I tapped the button on the earbud and ended the call. Now, all I had to do was give myself up and hope that would be enough of a distraction for Scarlett to get down to the safe room. It was hidden inside the house, impossible to find, and unless they had a bulldozer, they wouldn't be able to get into it.

I came around the front of the stairs and tossed my gun on the floor as the soldiers approached with their guns pointed in my face. But none of them fired, so at least their orders were to keep me alive.

Alive to torture me, no doubt.

They circled me and yanked my wrists behind my back like I was under arrest and secured the zip tie in place.

I wanted to ask questions, but I knew it wasn't their place to answer them.

They marched me forward toward the front doors, and just then, they swung inward, and the man Aldo had described stepped through, one hand in his pocket, a carefree energy about him. Instead of looking at me first, he got a lay of the land, looking at my floorplan before he was directly in front of me.

Then he finally looked at me.

Brown eyes in a hard face. In just a look, I could tell he was confident but not arrogant, that he was smart even though he hadn't spoken a word. Everyone possessed an energy that you could just feel—and I certainly felt his.

I bet he felt mine.

"I apologize for the fanfare. But you know how it goes." His voice was deep and possessed a hint of a French accent.

My blood started to boil because I knew who he was without knowing his name. "What do you want?"

"Let's start with an introduction." He looked away and scanned the room again. "I'm Draven—and I'm here to take the business." He turned his gaze back on me.

I needed him to focus on me, not the stairs. "I quit a while ago. I have nothing to offer you."

"Yes, I'm aware. Chosen to settle down in a quiet life with your lovely bride." He studied my expression, waiting for the rise of my anger. "And she is lovely, by the way. And her cooking..." His hand moved to his chest. "Phenomenal. And that means something coming from a French man."

I tested the zip ties, but they were locked tight.

His eyes lifted again.

I did what I had to do and decided to charge him.

He anticipated it and sidestepped me.

I lost my balance and hit the floor.

Two of his men lifted me and forced me upright.

But now his back was turned to the rest of the house, and the timing couldn't have been better because I spotted her making her way down the stairs. I yanked my gaze away and locked eyes with Draven, knowing any shift in my stare could give her away.

"That was elegant," he said with a slight smirk.

"I told you I'm not in the business anymore, so what the fuck do you want?"

"And I heard you the first time. But I need you for something."

"What?" I snapped. "Just tell me, and I'll do it." I couldn't care less about it, especially now that Dante wasn't a part of it. Draven could have the damn thing. The rest of us would be just fine without it.

His smile widened. "I wasn't expecting such enthusiastic cooperation."

"I just want you out of my fucking house. So what do you want?"

His hands slid into the pockets of his pants. "Theo. I want him here. Now."

The blood started to drain from my face. For a moment, I forgot about Scarlett when I realized my brother was the real target.

"From what I understand, you're very close."

*Fuck.*

"Call him. Tell him if he doesn't show up here in fifteen minutes, you'll get a bullet to the brain."

"I'm sure he would bow out if that's what you want."

"Really?" he asked, his tone suggesting he'd already explored that route. "Because we already had words, and he made it very clear, in no uncertain terms, that he would skin me alive and hang me from the Duomo for all to see if I stepped foot in his territory."

*Yep, that sounded like Theo.*

"I don't underestimate him. He's the Skull King for a reason. So the quickest way to end this is for you to make that call. One of you is going to die—him or you. Who do you think he'll choose?" He cocked his head slightly, a flash of mirth in his eyes, like this was child's play for him.

"Dante is the one who involved you. You should talk to him—"

"He's notified me of his retirement. I have my own production, but what I need is the distribution channels. And from what Dante has told me, Theo can move product like no other motherfucker."

"Even if you kill us both, the Skull Kings will come after you—"

"No, they won't," he said simply. "Not when I take his place. You'd be surprised how quickly loyalty can switch once they're on a commission scale rather than a salary. The Skull Kings will make far more than they ever have with me in charge." He nodded to one of his men.

He reached into my pocket and pulled out my phone. He opened the screen, found Theo's name, and held it up between us.

"Ready?" Draven asked.

I didn't know what the fuck to do. If I made that call, Theo would come, and he would be shot. And I wasn't entirely sure if Draven would let me go at that point. He might kill me anyway. Why hadn't Theo mentioned any of this to me?

The guy tapped the screen, put it on speaker, and then the phone started to ring.

*Please don't pick up...*

It rang and rang.

*Jesus Christ, don't pick up the phone.*

"Yeah?" Theo barked into the phone.

I closed my eyes in sheer disappointment. I'd never been more annoyed by the sound of his voice. One of the men kicked me, and I jerked as my eyes opened again.

Draven stood there, hands in his pockets, and watched.

"Axel, you there?"

"Yes, I'm here." I gave an irritated sigh.

"What's your deal?"

If I didn't have a wife, I knew I would just take the bullet and spare Theo. But I did have a wife, I did have a family, and if I died...she'd be alone. So I told him the truth. "Theo, you need to listen to me, alright?"

When he turned quiet, I knew he understood shit was real.

"I'm here with Draven."

Theo's reaction was an audible breath.

"I'm in zip ties. Not much I can do."

He didn't ask questions, didn't play his hand, and he didn't ask about Scarlett to protect her.

"I think you know where this is going."

He remained quiet.

"It's you or me—and I'm not sure which one you should pick."

Draven took the phone from his guy. "Come to Alexander's home in fifteen minutes—or I'll shoot him in the back of the head. It's that simple." He returned the phone to the space between us. "What's it going to be?"

Theo finally spoke. "He's got nothing to do with this—"

"Then come," Draven said simply. "Or make Scarlett into a young widow who will be my personal chef in Paris...in addition to her other duties."

Now the stakes had just gotten higher—and there wasn't a damn thing I could do about it. I wanted to beg Theo to come, not for me, but for my wife. But I kept my mouth shut. Even with Scarlett in that safe room, she wouldn't be protected from Draven forever. I didn't trust her father to do the job either.

Theo spoke again, his voice gruff with anger. "I'll be right there."

I needed that answer but also hated it. "Theo—"

"This is my fault, Axel. You chose to leave, so you shouldn't have to suffer because of my greed."

"You know he's probably going to kill me anyway."

Theo asked. "Hopefully not. But if he does, at least we go together."

Draven hit the button and ended the call. "That was touching—"

An explosion sounded outside, so loud it felt like we were in a war zone and a bomb had just gone off. It was so strong that the floor trembled beneath my feet, and I nearly fell over sideways.

Draven kept his cool as he turned toward the double doors while his men were deployed into action. Gunfire was audible a moment later. My guys must have bombed the gate to get through, and now they were taking down the enemy.

I felt a rush of pride.

Draven pulled out his pistol and pointed it at me, his stare suddenly vicious like he was a butcher with a knife and I was the lamb next up for slaughter. He stepped toward me, the gun steady in his hand, and then he grabbed me by the arm. "You think you're going anywhere." He shoved me forward so he could stand behind me, the gun pointed at my back. "When they get in here, you're going to order them to stand down."

I turned around to look at him. "After the threat you just made about my wife, I'd rather die. So, shoot me. I don't care, because they're going to shoot you, and that's all that matters."

He cocked the gun and gave a smirk. "Then maybe I will."

The sounds grew louder, like the threat was right outside the door and about to push in.

He raised the gun a little higher and steadied it on my face.

My heart raced with the uncertainty. I assumed the men would break through that door and take him out. Scarlett would be fine. But without actually seeing it with my own eyes, I would never know. But that was what I had to believe would happen if I were to die right there.

His fingers tightened over the trigger, and it looked like he was about to squeeze.

But then a bullet struck him from behind, hitting him in the back of his shoulder, and as he squeezed the trigger, the bullet missed me and hit the wall.

He grimaced before he gripped his shoulder then spun around to face his assailant.

It was Scarlett.

She stood there, her gun shaking in her hand, a little blood on her from the wound. "Drop your gun."

"You fucking cunt." He raised his gun, and I knew he wouldn't hesitate to shoot her.

"Baby, run!" I launched myself onto his back, knocking him clear to the floor and making his head slam into the marble. Without hands, I was almost useless, so it was quite the physical feat to roll over and kick the gun just out of his reach.

The doors popped open, and more gunfire ensued.

"Get down!" I yelled.

Scarlett dropped to the floor.

Draven moved for me and grabbed me by the neck, choking me hard before he threw his fist into my face. He hit me so hard, he broke my nose on the first punch. "I will relish this moment as I fuck your wife—"

I slammed my head into his face, stunning him for just a second.

Scarlett must have had her gun again, because a gun fired nearby, but it missed its target.

Then Draven was thrown off me, a heavy body coming to knock him flat onto his back.

Draven reacted quickly and punched his assailant. He moved fast, fighting like he had experience in the ring. He threw a punch and then a kick, knocking the gun from the other man's hand before kicking him in the face.

I realized it was Scarlett's father.

The two men went at it, neither having a weapon, both fighting with their fists and nothing else.

"Scarlett, don't shoot." I watched her train her gun on the fight, unsure when to pull the trigger to hit Draven and not her father. "There's a knife in my pocket. Cut me free."

She tossed the gun on the floor then dug her hand into my pocket, pulling out the big blade inside of the sheath. She pulled it free then cut my zip ties.

In that short amount of time, both men had landed substantial blows on each other. Dante was bleeding from the mouth, but so was Draven. Dante had to be fifteen years older, but he still held his own pretty well.

"Dad!"

I joined the fight, knocking into Draven's side and sending him across the floor.

Dante dove for the gun he'd dropped.

Draven stayed down for a second then spun his leg, catching my ankle and forcing me to flip down to the floor. Then he got on top of me, grabbed his dropped gun, and pointed it at me. He forced me up, using my body as a shield with the barrel against my temple.

Dante pointed his gun, but his hand shook.

Scarlett stood behind him, in a mess of tears.

"Let him go," Dante said in a strong voice.

The fight started to wind down. It was just a pile of bodies with lingering gunfire.

Draven continued to pull me back farther, back toward the staircase and the rest of the house. Then he let me go, the gun pointed at the back of my head. He took one step back then another. And then, once he was blocked by the wall, he took off and moved into the kitchen and the back part of the house.

Dante dropped his gun.

Scarlett ran straight to me and jumped into my arms, not caring about the blood that continued to pour down my face.

"Enough of this shit." Theo stepped inside with his shotgun and took out the remaining guys who still put up a fight.

It was silent after that, just the sound of Scarlett crying in my arms.

I held her against me, bleeding all over her, and just breathed. Breathed because it was over—and it was over because she'd saved my life. She always had my back, even if it meant risking her own life. I squeezed her and cherished her in a way I never had until that moment.

"Sweetheart, are you alright?" I knew Dante couldn't stay away. Needed to interfere with our embrace because his daughter meant more to him than our affection.

She left my arms and ran to him next. "Dad!"

I felt cold the moment she was gone.

Dante gripped her hard and cupped the back of her head. His eyes were immediately wet with tears that had been ready to fall for weeks. "Oh, sweetheart." He closed his eyes as he held her, getting blood in her hair.

"Did you get him?" Theo came to my side, his eyes throbbing with pure malice.

"He ran off."

Theo motioned for his men to follow.

"There's a small gate in the back corner," I said. "He probably shot off the lock and ran for it."

"We'll find that motherfucker." His hand moved to my shoulder, looking at my broken nose. "You alright?"

"I'm fine." My eyes traveled to Scarlett and Dante, who continued to hold each other in a happy reunion. "She's fine, so I'm fine."

"I'm sorry I got you mixed up in this."

"It's not your fault." I continued to look at Dante. "It's his, remember? He's the one who looped in that French bastard in the first place."

"Yeah, but I kinda stirred the pot...a bit. Something I'm known to do."

"You think he'll be a problem again?"

"No." Theo withdrew his arm. "Because I'm going to kill that motherfucker before he heads back to France. If he makes it out of here, he'll be heading to his private plane at the airport, and there's only one airport around here, so he won't be hard to find."

"Good luck."

He pointed at his face. "Good luck with that broken nose. You look like shit."

"Fuck you."

He grinned before he walked off. "Fuck you too."

Scarlett and Dante finally broke apart.

"I'm sorry for everything," Dante said. "Truly, I am."

"I know. I know you are."

Dante had a light in his eyes, a joy in his expression that defied all the bloodshed that had just happened. "So...are we okay?" He seemed to hold his breath as he waited for her answer.

She nodded, new tears emerging in her eyes.

Dante's looked the same. "That makes me...very happy."

After Scarlett hugged her father again, she turned back to me. "Oh, your nose."

"It's fine. I don't even notice it."

"Are you alright?"

I pressed a kiss to her temple as I pulled her close. "I'm alright because of you. Nice shot."

"Told you I knew how to use a gun," she said with a slight smile.

I smiled back before I looked at Dante. "I'm alright because of you, too. Got here just in time." I extended my hand to shake his.

He took it. "I'm glad you're alright, Axel. I'm glad everyone is alright."

I squeezed her into me again and kissed her temple. "Me too."

"Your beautiful house is destroyed," she said sadly.

"*Our* house," I said. "And it's fine. We'll go on our honey-moon while it's being fixed."

"Ooh..." She kept her cheek against my chest. "I guess something good did come out of all of this."

# Chapter 20

## *Scarlett*

I was working in the back office doing paperwork when Alessandra walked in.

"Your father is here to see you. Wants to know if you're free for lunch?"

"Oh, tell him I'll be right there." I finished up my work then closed my laptop before I walked to the lobby. He was there, dressed nicely and looking handsome as ever, just with a slight bruise on his face. "Hey, Dad."

"Hey, sweetheart. Would you like to have lunch?"

I had a lot of work to do, but that didn't seem important anymore. "Sure. Where do you want to go?"

He gestured to the tables behind him. "Where else?"

"We don't have to eat here, Dad."

"I love it."

My eyes narrowed.

"Honestly."

"Well, it would be quicker than going somewhere else." I grabbed two menus from the hostess stand, and we walked to a table together. Lunchtime was much slower than dinnertime, so we condensed our menu during the day to just the more popular lunch items, like salads, sandwiches, and soups.

He pulled out the chair for me and sat across from me, straightening his collared shirt the way he always did. He opened the menu and looked, and it seemed to take him only a second to decide what he wanted.

"Let me guess...the Caesar?"

He smirked. "I'd like to try those focaccia croutons."

"They're house-made."

"Yes, I saw that on the menu."

The waiter came over, took our drink order and, since we were ready for lunch, also took our food order. A moment later, he returned with our wine and let us enjoy it.

My father stared at his wine for a while before he looked at me, visibly awkward for some reason.

"What is it?"

He gave a shrug. "This is nice, is all."

"It is nice."

"I'm grateful we get to have this." He gave me a soft smile, his affection written all over his face.

"Me too." He didn't deserve my forgiveness, but he'd earned it through tragedy, tragedy that put everything in perspective. If he hadn't stormed those doors in time, my husband would have died...and I probably would have died too. "So, you're seeing Hannah?"

Instead of skirting the question or avoiding it altogether, he answered it head on. "Yes. There's always been this... energy...between us. There were times when I felt like she was trying to make something happen, but I avoided those compromising situations. Mixing business and pleasure is never a good idea, so it wasn't an option. But now..." He gave a shrug. "It is an option."

"And it does work sometimes...like it did with Axel and me."

"Yes, you're right about that."

"So you like her?"

He didn't seem uncomfortable with the questions, maybe because he was just thrilled that we were having a conversation at all. "I do. She's always been so good to me and knows me so well. And she's very beautiful..."

"She's got one hell of an ass on her."

My dad smirked then darted his eyes away, deeply embarrassed by that comment.

"I'm happy for you."

"You are?" he asked. "I know she's a bit younger than me..."

"*A bit?*" I asked with a laugh.

"Okay, more than a bit. But it works. And I'm glad that you're supportive of this relationship."

"I just want you to be happy, Dad. You deserve to have someone, and I've noticed the way Hannah has looked at you for years. It's not like you were a creep that came on to her. I think she'd been into you for a long time."

"Perhaps."

"Does she want a family?"

"I imagine so."

"And how do you feel about that? You're still young enough."

He released a sarcastic chuckle. "I don't know about that."

"You were fist-fighting a guy fifteen years younger than you."

"When your life is on the line, you'd be surprised at what you can do. But the lack of sleep and the diapers and the baby shit everywhere... I don't know. And besides, I have you, and I'm really not interested in having another child. I have the daughter I've always wanted. I've loved every stage of being your father, but this is the one I'm enjoying the most, because I get to be your friend."

"It is nice."

"So, no more children for me."

"Well, then I guess Hannah won't be around long."

"I don't know. She's never told me whether she wants children. Perhaps she doesn't. If she wants to be with me, perhaps she knows that dating an older man means a child-free life makes more sense. We'll see," he said with a shrug. "And what about you?"

"We want children."

"It's a long and exhausting journey, but when you reach the top and see the view...it's all worth it."

I smiled. "Axel kinda wants them now, but I'm not ready yet."

"What's the rush?"

"I don't know. He's just excited by the idea."

"You have time, sweetheart. Enjoy your husband and your freedom, because once you have kids, it'll be gone forever." He reached for his wineglass and took a drink. "I lost a lot of friends and opportunities, having you so young. Would I change anything? No. But it does alter things."

"So...do you really know nothing about my mother?"

The question made him tighten in discomfort. His eyes immediately dropped to his wineglass. "Why do you ask?"

"I'm just curious."

"If I could use my resources to exonerate Axel, I don't see why I can't use them to track her down...if that's what you want." He swirled his wineglass and took a drink.

"Do you think she regrets her decision?" I asked. "Now that she's older? Now that she probably does have children?"

"I can't speak for her. But if she could see you now, she would definitely know she missed out on something special." His eyes lifted from the wine, and he gave me a soft smile.

I smiled back. "Thanks, Dad."

---

I walked into my old apartment, finding Axel on the couch in nothing but his sweatpants. While our home was being renovated and cleansed of bullet holes, we'd decided it was easiest to stay here. Aldo remained to oversee the project while we focused on the restaurant.

Axel turned off the TV and came toward me, a mountain with his height and muscles. "How was work?"

"The restaurant is doing well."

"I know it is." He smirked before he kissed me. "But I still like hearing you say it."

"Way to give it a rest."

"I'll never give it a rest." He looked down at the bag of takeout food I had in my hand. "You got something for me?" Now he wore a full grin, just as excited for food as he was for sex.

I set it on the counter. "I thought you might be hungry."

"Baby, you know me so well." His hand moved around my waist, and of course, his hand crept down to my ass and gave it a hard squeeze. He kissed my temple before he pulled away and took the container out of the bag.

"My father stopped by. We had lunch."

"Nice." He grabbed a fork from the drawer then sat on the couch to eat straight out of the container. "How's he doing?"

"Good. Told me he and Hannah are officially a thing."

"Like he hasn't been boning her for years."

"He said he hadn't."

"Sure." He took a big bite and chewed.

"Anyway, it was nice. Nice to talk to him like a friend."

He watched me as he ate, hanging on to my words like they were fascinating.

"A part of me feels stupid for letting it go, but...I don't know."

"You're happy, right?"

"Yes."

"Then it doesn't matter," he said. "If he pulls something again, that's a different story. But I know he won't." He continued to eat, devouring the half-moon raviolis in a butter-cream sauce.

"So, did Theo ever catch Draven?"

"Don't worry about it," he said. "You don't need to waste your time thinking about that stuff."

"So, that's a no."

"Like I said, don't worry about it."

"He tried to kill my husband and my brother-in-law—"

"Who hasn't?" he asked with a smirk. "I really don't want you to worry your pretty little head over this. Theo knows what he's doing."

After something so traumatic, it was hard to ever let it go, but it was a waste of life to spend it worrying about death.

"Did you make this?" he asked. "It's better than what the chefs make."

"You can tell?" I asked in slight surprise.

"Definitely," he said. "I can always tell the difference because I can taste the love."

"That's sweet."

He finished the contents and closed the box before he set it aside. "So, I have something to tell you." He moved from his seat to sit beside me.

"This sounds like good news."

"Oh, it is," he said. "I booked us a two-week honeymoon to Santorini."

That sounded divine...but two weeks? "That's kinda a long time."

Both of his eyebrows rose. "Sex with me for two weeks sounds like a long time?"

"I only meant with the restaurant. We *just* opened it."

"Alessandra has it covered."

"I—I don't know..." I felt irresponsible walking away from a brand-new business so quickly. "Maybe a week—"

"Baby, it'll be fine. You think the place is going to burn down?"

"I just know that the quality of restaurants diminishes when the owner isn't around."

"So, your plan was to never take a vacation?"

"I didn't say that. Just not right now—"

"We're going," he said. "Period."

I rolled my eyes. "You can't just tell me what to do—"

"Well, I just did. So pack your shit because we're leaving tomorrow."

I rolled my eyes, but truth be told, I couldn't be that angry. Looking out at the Mediterranean Sea with my gorgeous husband beside me...that sounded pretty great. Romantic dinners, late nights between the sheets, shower sex—it all sounded great. "Well, if we're leaving tomorrow, I better start packing."

He grinned. "That's my baby."

# Epilogue

## Axel

Theo was the last to arrive, and he arrived with a gift, tissue paper sticking up from the top. He looked out of place carrying it, like someone was holding him at gunpoint.

"You made it. Finally." I clapped him on the shoulder. "What's this?"

"A gift." He set it on the table where the other presents were. "Isn't that what you're supposed to do at this sort of thing?"

"It's a gender reveal, so no. What did you get?"

"Diapers," he said. "And I wrote that you're an idiot on all of them. Something to read in the middle of the night."

I grinned. "Thanks, man."

Dante was already there with Hannah, and my parents were there too. Scarlett stood in a dress and heels, her large stomach noticeable in the baggy fabric. She was talking to her father, who had his arm around Hannah, and Scarlett was rubbing her stomach absent-mindedly like she always did.

"Nervous?" Theo asked.

"Why would I be nervous?"

"I'd be nervous as fuck if I were going to be a father."

"I'm excited, man."

"You know what the sex is?"

"Nope. Aldo is the only one who knows."

Theo crossed his arms over his chest. "What do you think it is?"

I shrugged.

"What do you hope it is?"

"I honestly don't care. Boy or girl, doesn't matter to me."

"Well, I think it's a boy."

"Why?" I asked.

He shrugged. "Look at how big she is. That's obviously a big boy."

"Did you just call my wife fat?"

He smirked. "I would never."

Scarlett came over and hugged Theo. "So glad you came. And you brought a gift."

"Diapers," he said. "No idea if they're the right size."

She smiled. "Whatever the size, the baby will fit into them eventually." She rubbed her dress over her stomach, arching her back more than she used to, to accommodate the extra weight. It was harder for her to get around, so our nights were spent in front of the TV with me rubbing her feet or her back. She didn't cook anymore, and she'd stopped going into the restaurant for the time being. But despite her discomfort, she was very excited. "Now that everyone's here, ready to find out if we're having a boy or a girl?"

"I'm ready." Theo looked at me. "What about you?"

"I've been ready since the day she told me she was pregnant." My arm moved around her waist, and we walked to the cake on the kitchen island. Aldo had ordered it from her favorite bakery, and the inside was colored pink for a girl or blue for a boy.

"Oh my god, I'm so nervous," she said.

Her father and Hannah gathered around with my parents, all of whom were equally excited about their first grandchild.

I grabbed the cake knife and handed it to her. "Would you like to do the honors, baby?"

"I don't know. I'm so nervous."

"Here." I had her take the end of the handle. "Just hold it." I grabbed the handle closer to the blade and did it for her, having her hold on and let the knife move on its own. We sliced into the soft frosting and the layers below. The shadow in the crack was still too dark to distinguish anything, so we made another cut on the other side.

"I don't see any color yet," Dante said.

Mom gave a sigh. "Hurry up. We need to know."

I cut the other side then slid the knife underneath the base to lift it in the air.

Blue.

"Oh my god, we're having a boy!" Scarlett threw her hands over her face and, like a spark to a match, burst into tears. "We're having a boy."

I returned the slice to the table and wrapped my arms around her. "These tears of sadness or joy?"

"Neither." She sobbed into my chest. "I'm just...I don't know." She'd been a lot more emotional lately. We were watching TV one night, and a cat commercial came on and made her bawl.

I kissed her temple. "I'm excited to have a little man running around the house."

Everyone cheered in excitement. My mom hugged my father, and they cherished the moment.

Dante smiled. "A grandson...I like that."

Theo drank from his scotch. "I just hope he's nothing like you, Axel. He could look identical to Scarlett, and you'd still be uglier."

"Thanks, man." I kissed my wife again.

He raised his glass. "Anytime."

Scarlett continued to sob into my arms. "Can you believe it?"

My hand went to her distended stomach and bunched the fabric under my fingertips. "I'm so excited. I never cared about being a father before you. But now, it's a dream come true."

"You're so sweet. I hope he's just as sweet."

"I'm sure he will be. A big mama's boy."

"That would be nice." She stopped crying, her makeup smeared from the tears. "I just hope he's not close to your size because that's gonna be rough."

"You can do it, baby."

"Easy for you to say. You don't have to do it."

"You know I would if I could." I pulled her in again and gave her a kiss.

She left my arms and went over to each guest one at a time, hugging them and thanking them for being a part of this special moment. My parents were always happy to talk to her, and without their telling me how they felt toward her, I knew they loved her.

Dante left Hannah's side and came to mine. "Congratulations."

"Congratulations to you."

"Thank you," he said. "I'm very excited. And if you need a babysitter, call me."

"You?" I asked incredulously.

"I raised a little girl all on my own, didn't I?" He nodded toward her. "And look how she turned out."

"True," I said with a smile. "I'll keep that in mind."

He patted me on the back. "Thank you for everything. I know this moment wouldn't be possible without the way you supported my relationship with Scarlett. Most men wouldn't have tolerated me, probably would have killed me, but you had the grace to forgive me. You're a very admirable man, and if my grandson is anything like you, he'll be a fine man indeed."

My eyes shifted away in discomfort. His words were appreciated, but the sentiment made me feel all sorts of things that were unwelcome. "Thank you for saying that."

"Of course," he said. "We're a family."

I nodded as I continued to watch Scarlett, making my father laugh with something cute she said. "Yeah...we're a family."

---

## Next in the series...

My husband of two years tells me he wants an open marriage.

I'm stunned. I'm hurt. And I'm livid. I don't want to be married to a man who wants to open our bed to other people.

But then I get a flat tire in the pouring rain and a sexy-as-hell gentleman helps me out.

My husband is in the game, so one look at the skull ring on this gentleman's left hand tells me exactly who he is.

The Skull King.

I didn't want an open marriage...but I definitely want this man.

**<u>Order Now</u>**

Printed in Great Britain
by Amazon

43524007R00219